WHITE POPPIES

WHITE POPPIES

VIVIEN JONES

Published by
Pewter Rose Press
Nottingham, NG2 6EY
United Kingdom
www.pewter-rose-press.com

First published in Great Britain 2012
© Vivien Jones 2012
ISBN 978-1908136312

British Library Cataloguing in Publication Data
A catalogue record for this book is available from the British Library

The author acknowledges support from a Creative Scotland Writer's Bursary
Cover image by Helen Lowther

ALBA | CHRUTHACHAIL

A Woman's Handbook for Dealing with War
A collection of flash fictions and short stories of women
amongst warriors

Author's note

I was born in 1948 into a Naval family – both parents served in the second world war in the Royal Navy, my father until he retired. Naturally, the moment I turned fourteen I became a pacifist, a member of CND and any other liberal/left/ revolutionary group that would let me in. Later Amnesty and the broad feminist movement became my intellectual and moral resting place. Although I disagreed on principle with much of what my parents believed in, I loved the stories they told of their lives in the war, and it is these anecdotes and my own experience of protest and pacifism, along with a love of history, that have inspired this exploration of women amongst warriors. From the mythical (Valkyries) to the historical (Romans and Renaissance events), to huge changes in attitudes through the twentieth century, the stories animate some of those experiences.

Contents

...heroes coming from the world

...What kind of a dream is it, said Óðinn,
in which just before daybreak,
I thought I cleared Valhǫll,
for coming of slain men?
I waked the Einherjar,
bade valkyries rise up,
to strew the bench,
and scour the beakers,
wine to carry,
as for a king's coming,
here to me I expect
certain great ones,
so glad is my heart.

Three ravens rose in a black spiral towards the full moon. When their bodies crossed the disc their ragged feathers turned to silk trailers. When they emerged from the other side they were Valkyrie again, Skuld, Gunnr and Hildr, three of the six most ancient choosers of the slain. They flew to a barren mountain top and landed noisily with a great deal of clattering of spears and armour. They were not in a good mood.

Gunnr (*War* in Norse) spoke first. 'I say we recalculate. In the same sense as their sat-navs do. We have lost our way and must find it again.'

Skuld (*Future* in Norse) spoke next. 'But we cannot move the goal-posts, as their politicians say. We are bound to Odin's command.'

Hildr, (*Battle* in Norse) added, 'But Odin could not anticipate the numbers we are having to deal with. The others Skögul, Göndul and Geirskögul have withdrawn their labour. They wish to renegotiate the guidelines.'

Skuld and Gunnr looked at her, appalled.

'Yes, they want to restrict entry to Valhalla to those who fight by hand. They claim that button pushing does not constitute courage. Nor satellite-assisted target-setting, nor the use of missiles with on-board computers. They claim it's giving war – sorry Gunnr – a bad name. And there aren't enough of us to go round.'

The three fell silent, each trawling her memory in search of the moment when their own task started to get complicated.

Gunnr was inclined to blame the Gatling gun, their year 1861, which automated killing and made redundant the skill of appropriate selection of a man to fight. She did not count field cannon which as often killed the firers as the enemy. She felt the same about grapeshot, an indiscriminate mess of a weapon. In the American Civil War, so numerous were the dead, the Valkyries had had to adopt a sample system. They searched for the places where the dead had defended themselves, accepting that it must have taken courage to try to beat off a Gatling gun with a rifle.

Skuld put it down to the AK-47 and its proliferation, their year 1947. That such a simple, effective weapon should find its way into the hands of every army, established and revolting, ambitious criminals in the world and terrorists or freedom fighters who between them had made battlegrounds of every corner of the earth. The Valkyries' duty to visit battlegrounds and choose the worthy slain was problematic.

It was hard defining battleground when swathes of current warfare happened in guerrilla format. Skuld had never admired the sneakiness of the sniper's work even if the other side was better armed and more numerous. Battle was a meeting of equals, with conquest the result of skill, courage and determination of one warrior over another. Nothing so simple since the arrival of the AK-47, whose inventor would rather have come up with lawnmowers. Well, he did in a way, Skuld thought, and the men were the grass.

Hildr remained of the opinion that it was the definition of weapons that had complicated their duties. Her notion was that where there was bloodshed there was a sense of responsibility, and therefore some humanity. She found the use of chemical weapons, designed and tested in peaceful rural laboratories, incomprehensible. That a weapon could poison land, civilians, animals and finally, randomly, some soldiers, robbed her of her ability to discriminate any sense of courage amongst the victims. They simply looked terrified, choked, burnt, blistered, in spasm, in their own melting body fluids. She had thought perhaps that the warriors who were tested upon must have shown courage, but then she discovered that they had not been told by the authorities what was happening. If the results were too visible or distressing they were given money. After the judicial report. She thought the mustard gas of their first World War had been an escalation in the scale of it. Where it would end – perhaps with a poisoned planet – she could not tell – but there would be little need of Valkyries in a final battle of toxins.

There had already been many discussions; they had mulled over these things before, alone and together. At the time of the automation of weapons a great gathering of

Valkyries had been called to Valhalla by Odin himself, to consider the implications of impersonal mass slaughter on the battlefield, and the simultaneous proliferation of battlefields. He was no less angry now.

'We must modernise!' Odin thundered.

Only Gunnr dared to say, 'If this is the direction of modern warfare we may be headed for obsolescence.'

'Explain!' commanded Odin.

'At your order, we have only concerned ourselves with warriors on the battlefield. We brought the courageous here to wait for Ragnarök when the Gods will fall. But men now fight machines or machines fight machines and men merely point them at each other. I ask, are we concerned with warriors or with courage? If Valhalla is to be filled with the brave, might we look elsewhere on the battlefield?'

Odin considered this. 'Go on,' he said.

'I have seen courage in many others. Now that we have the internet and can see all the world's battles, I have seen many medical people, ambulance drivers, nurses and doctors all working without proper supplies under fire. I have seen aid workers doing the same. And the very people who film these events, they show courage too.'

Odin shook his head. For the first time he looked at Gunnr and spoke directly to her. She did not flinch though his eyes were flinty.

'What use will doctors and nurses and photographers be here? We are preparing for The Twilight of the Gods, the last battle, the flood.'

'And after The Flood?'

'I shall be dead. What does it matter to me?'

12

'Not everyone will be dead. The world will need makers and thinkers. What if the two survivors were two warriors? Wouldn't they just fall to fighting? But if they were a maker and thinker – much more interesting for the reborn Gods...'

Odin sighed. 'A world without me...' he said, his tone tragic. 'So we must now recalculate.'

Gunnr tuned her spear to the internet and watched the image appear on her shield. The others gathered round. They flicked across the world, file-shared, made friends, linked and tagged until they had accumulated the first thousand brave, accidental, dead participants in the day's battle. These they uploaded to Valhalla where a rather awkward Odin bade them welcome, storing their first aid kits and cameras in the halls where once there were only weapons.

Then the Three Wise Valkyries, rose into the sky, crossed the moon and were ravens once more.

Tancorix And The Wall

Old Carlisle Fort: Tombstone
TANCORIX MVLIER VIGSIT ANNOS SEGSAGINTA
"Tancorix a wife, who lived for sixty years."

80 AD

You, Tancorix – love a soldier? A Roman soldier?

I told you, Father – he's not a born Roman – he's from Gaul. He hates them as much as we do. You know the situation. You convert or you die. So he converted and was sent here. Don't you believe me, Father?

What's he doing on the Wall then? Who's he guarding it against?

No-one – he doesn't bother – nothing ever happens up there. He's been there for three years. It's not even a mile-castle, just a turret at the top of a steep bank. What he mostly sees are rabbits.

Some soldier!

Let me tell you how it happened.

I'd been gathering early and taken my fruit to Banna, to the path-side where the soldiers pass on their way to the fort. The berries were fat and juicy and my basket was full. It was busy that day, there was a group of weavers come up from Luguvalium with their summer's work – winter starts early on the Wall and they were doing good trade. An argument broke out between two soldiers. They both had hold of a piece of cloth and they were pulling against each other so hard that one of them lost his grip and he toppled back into me. I dropped my basket and the berries went everywhere.

The fallen soldier swore at me then picked up a handful of fruit. I thought he was going to rub it in my face. That's when the other soldier stepped in. He caught the rough one by the arm and twisted him round to face him.

'Leave her. She did nothing.'

'Piss off, Gaul!' he snarled, but he moved out of the way and became very interested in some pots across the path.

So that was the first time I saw Dorios – that's his own name – the Romans at the fort call him Aquila. It means 'eagle' – that makes him laugh, but not in his eyes. Anyway, he helped me gather the fruit from the dust but it was only good for mashing, if that. When he saw my tears he pressed a coin into my hand, more than enough for the wasted fruit.

Then he said did I know the Wall at all?

He had such a good face under that helmet.

I said I did.

From Banna, it's very nearly a day's walk. I knew the way because I'd once travelled to the mile-station with Father, delivering ale. I told them I was going to search for new berry fields, there are sloes and red berries up that way. I knew I wouldn't be back that night but I didn't tell Father. I knew where I hoped to spend the night. He had such a good face.

We talked all night. Tucked inside the small square of the turret with his new blanket round our shoulders. Every now and then he stood to peer into the night – so he did watch over the bare landscape – but he soon squatted beside me again. He told me about his home in Gaul, a steading among other steadings, about the animals, about his mother and sisters, about the coming of the Romans, the killing of his father. He had thrown himself at them with as big a stick as he could carry. They had laughed at him, disarmed him, boxed his ears. Instead of killing him too, because he showed spirit, they took him with them. His mother's cries had echoed in his dreams for months. Then he listened to me.

He knew little of Cartimandua, Queen of Brigantes and a warrior – how we Carvetii feared her and hated her closeness to the Romans, how we hoped, when she took Venutius for husband he might persuade her away from their patronage. Venutius is Carvetii. I told Dorios of the great gathering when Venutius walked out, with Cartimandua cursing him from her wagon, swearing she would send Romans after him. You said no, she would never turn on our tribe, on her own husband. But she did. Venutius is hiding even now among the Novantae to the West, with the tribe that threatened the Wall. Dorios, for all his watching, has never seen a Novantae. There was one, wasn't there Father, who passed through Banna last year but he was no warrior. A bard, I think. He carried a harp.

The Romans say they are farmers, little else, and not worth conquering. Dorios doesn't always believe what they tell him. He thinks they tell the soldiers, especially the converts, as little as possible.

Father – we think to join Venutius and his followers in the West. Dorios will be valuable to the tribe whether he farms or soldiers. The Romans will not venture there – it is too far west of the wall, too costly to build forts. They do not want the country so he will be safe.

Give us your blessing, Father. I will miss you so.

99 AD

Tancorix, is it you?

They told me you are ill, Father, and soon to die.

They hope. I am not dying, just a chill.

I have been waiting so long. How did you come to Banna?

I came with the bard. No-one knows we are here. And is this Dorios beside you?

This is our son. He is fourteen, a man nearly. His name is Calgacus.

A great name.

A great man, a great speaker.

I heard him speak against the Romans.

That was many years ago.

And you with the Novantae, allies with the Romans.

Not at all. Father, do not agitate yourself.

Then tell me, Tancorix. Bring the boy close. Tell me what happened.

We had heard that there was a great farm camp well to the West. Dorios changed clothing with a weaver so that nothing remained of his Roman gear. The weaver seemed to like his new clothes enough to risk an encounter with a Roman patrol. It was not so great a risk. Many of the soldiers barter their clothing for anything that takes their fancy. They're not supposed to do it but no-one can stop it.

It took us seven days to reach our destination. We avoided the Roman way-stations, keeping to the valleys where we could. It was autumn and cold and by the time we came to our destination I was in a sorry state, shivering and burning by turns. Dorios was near carrying me by then but the squealing of pigs and cries of cattle all round made me open my eyes to see a marvellous sight.

We were standing between the uprights of a timber gateway that broke through high ramparts circling a space as big as the market in Luguvalium. There were three great roundhouses, all with smoking chimneys and animals all round, sheep and fowl as well as the pigs and cows. We were strangers, dirty and hungry with nothing to trade.

We were taken to their leader, a man named Brenn, who said little but listened intently as some other elders questioned us. At some point he gave a slight nod and the questioning ended. We were welcomed, not least for our determination in getting there on foot from near Luguvalium. Their whispering together did not seem hostile. They could see that Dorios was strong and that we could both be useful workers. Soon they drew us close to the hearth and told us where we were.

This was Rispain, an ancient farm so well suited to the land it had been farmed as far into memory as living minds could stretch. Not even the oldest knew of a time before its building, no mention of it in tales or songs from their parents but they all knew of its strength and wealth. In clear weather from the ramparts you could see the waters that flow from the great sea all the way here. So many times I dreamed of sailing home on that water. Especially in the early days when we had to prove our worth.

At first Dorios was sent to work and guard another farm that looked over the sea from a high cliff. It was called Barsalloch and exposed to the wildest of storms. Venutius, the fugitive warrior, was its master. From his cliff-top viewpoint, Venutius kept urgent watch for the approach of Roman ships, knowing their and his wife's relentless will to punish. He was consumed with anger at having to live in this wild landscape when he was the husband of a Queen. Dorios found him arrogant. I would have liked to speak to another exiled Carvetii but I had to stay at Rispain and take up work as a brewer's assistant. The farm grew barley enough to make beer, which was so strong it took possession of some of the men's brains, so it was wise to stay quiet in a dark corner when they drank. The other women were not yet friendly and I longed to see Dorios.

Our proving time was short enough, a season. We did not know that they sent the bard on one of his constant spying missions to find out about us, nor that he reported back some months later that our story was true. On his return, Dorios was summoned to Rispain and we were reunited and given sleeping space together. He shared guard duties with the other men but most of the time he spent in hunting deer for the farm.

Because he moved about the countryside Dorios became a trusted man who carried and received messages from far off tribes. Brenn, our leader, summoned him often and sent him to the settlement at Locopibium, where travellers met and talked. When he heard tales of another Roman wall in the making, this time well to the north of us, Brenn asked him to take the boys and young men and teach them what military arts he knew in case the Romans would try to occupy our land. A northern wall would cut us off from tribes beyond, as the eastern one separated us, apart from secret forays, from my own tribe. Calcagus was born into this worried time. Brenn sent word to the tribes inside the two Roman walls that they too should prepare their communities. He sent watchers to where the Romans maintained camps, even though the Roman camps were small and mainly in place to control what little trading took place. Brenn watched those camps for signs of enlargement aware that it might be a signal of nothing beyond keeping Roman soldiers busy in an empty valley. But he continued to be wary.

There was a meeting, so many torches, so much clanking of iron, a steaming mass of horses tethered where the cattle usually lay and much food to prepare. They made a contract. They called themselves the Maeatae and vowed to resist any Roman incursion. It was exciting and frightening to listen to their loud boastful shouts.

That night Dorios was vexed. He said the loudest shouts came from those who had never fought the Romans. He thought that it was good to prepare but better to avoid conflict. The Romans were better armed, better trained and had countless men at their command. Remembering his own childhood experience he could imagine Rispain burning, the stock stolen, the people killed, enslaved or driven away. I could imagine Dorios executed, Calgacus taken and made a Roman, and me made a soldier's whore. We swore to persuade others of this terrible outcome of any battle, each in our own way.

He asked Brenn if there were those who might talk to the Romans, find their intentions, see if there were ways of avoiding battle. He could not be among them, his fugitive status would stay with him forever, but he thought it unlikely that the Romans would covet territory with few people or roads. Venutius opposed this strategy, claiming there could be no treaty with Romans, no agreement that they would not break if they stood to gain power. He and Dorios argued back and forth while Brenn listened, giving no indication of his thoughts, supporting neither man but listening intently to the debate.

I spoke softly to the wives and mothers as we worked. There were a great number of children in the farm and though they worked daily beside their mothers, they also played and listened to songs and stories until they fell asleep where they lay. Because food was abundant that year there was little need for them to forage, except for the love of being in the forest or out in the hills. The children conducted rowdy mushroom hunts with a wise woman in tow to identify poison among the collection. The older boys counted the days before they would be released from stock herding and allowed to go with the hunters. The girls learnt to weave or brew, one or two seeking plant knowledge and the art of healing, a few patient enough to catch fish from the river. The farm had been free of disease, in stock and people, for several years. There was time for singing and dancing and many babies were made and many survived their first year. It was a good time in the farm, a good time to speak of ways of protecting us all.

No woman sees her son as a warrior in her heart. Cuts and bruises, fevers, broken limbs and accidents account for all too many young lives. To survive childhood, for a son to be slain as a warrior, is the stuff of her nightmares rather than dreams. All the talk and tales of glory and courage surging around the night fires fell on deaf ears among the women, especially the widows and mothers of dead sons. Each woman whispered to her man. Each man had cause for thought.

And did they come – the Romans? I heard nothing.

No, Father – we were not worth their attentions.

But it sounds so good.

We are too far away. Too small.

So, you are at peace?

A watchful peace. Brenn is a wise man.

And Venutius? Was he contained?

Venutius? He left. Said we were rabbits to his wolf. Went to wage war on Cartimandua. It was all he thought about.

She shamed her tribe.

His rage was personal.

The betrayal of Caratacus? But to give a warrior to the Romans. Caratacus was seeking sanctuary.

He might have said that was his reason. It was much more personal.

The soldier husband?

Venutius was a proud man. A general. To be exiled and have his bed taken by a common soldier. He was stung. She wanted power. She could not fight the Romans so she joined them. Some people might think we did the same.

You avoided that? They offer only subservience or enmity.

We found a way to suffer one another – an unequal alliance – we vowed not to plot and they left us alone. We were not worth bothering with. What had we but farms and wilderness? For all their cleverness they are blind to wealth other than gold.

And Dorios? Is he well?

He eludes them still. I doubt that any of the soldiers we see remember that once a runaway fled the wall with a Carvetii maid. But he remains careful. He absents himself hunting in the woods if Romans are in the area. He made us travel here in secret.

You are still in danger then?

I doubt it. Do I still look like the wild daughter that ran away?

She was a girl. You are a woman.

I said we would travel in secret so that he would not worry.

A good thing. Romans have long memories. They are keen on their idea of justice.

I was never a fugitive. And they don't know of Calgacus.

I didn't know of Calgacus. Come closer, boy. Let me look at you. You look like your father. I only saw him once, the night you fled, but he was striking enough. I'm weary now. I will sleep. Tancorix, take the boy and feed yourselves. How long will you stay?

Two or three nights. I will come again when you have slept.

That's good.

...but he died in his sleep that night, Dorios. I had so much more to tell him. They took his body to Maglona, his birthplace. I couldn't be there to bury him so close to the military fort. His friends told me what happened after we fled so long ago. The Romans interrogated him, threw him in a cell and beat him. He told them we had fled to the East and they sent a marching patrol after us. Then they beat him again when they didn't find us. He endured all this to keep me safe. I'm so glad he saw Calgacus.

Promise me this, Dorios, when I die you'll take me home to lie beside him. It won't matter to me whether I look over the fields of Rispain or of Wiza Beck, only that it's not a battleground.

Three Last Thoughts

Eve of The Battle of Flodden 1513.
James IV, King of Scotland takes on the forces of Henry VIII
of England.

Janet Bairars, sometime mistress of James IV, in Whithorn.

It seems forever since I was here last. Six years. That great
company all gathered to give thanks for the birth of a baby.
One hundred and twenty miles from Edinburgh. I used to
think Jamie was over-pious. Now I've walked it too for the
same reason. Forgiveness. Intervention. Pity. I'm here to pray
for them all, for my husband and Jamie and all those men
who've left their families to follow their King. No petty
Highland jaunt this time. They're for fighting the English. Six
years. That fool Damian making bird wings out of hen
feathers. Brave enough to try and thrawn enough to survive
the drop. And only a limp to show for it. Six years. All those
prayers and yet the wee Prince died. Lived for a year and
that's worse, far worse, than the ones that died at birth. There
were four of them too weak to live. She nearly died herself
with each birth. So there's Prince James who's nearly a year,
and another on the way. And Jamie preparing to go to war
and then a crusade. She's about demented they tell me, her
husband going to fight her brother, half her servants on one
side and half on the other. Her brother, young Henry Tudor.
A dancer and a ladies' man, a peacock not a soldier. Jamie is
a soldier above all other things.

I never had a living child yet. Not for want of trying.
Perhaps I'm cursed for being Jamie's wanton. And now

Drummond has taken the men to join Jamie at Linlithgow, before they're headed for the border.

Jamie used to say I had the second sight. That's why I came here. I have a bad feeling in my heart that Drummond will never be a father. Miracles happen here so I've come to pray to Saint Ninian for them all.

Jamie, Drummond and Margaret too.

Poor lady, she'll be torn in two by all this.

Ford Castle, September 1513

My dearest wife,

I stay briefly with Lady Heron at this border keep. No great comforts here, but we must secure our passage home before the battle. Surrey is to lead the English. So, I meet a knight and a worthy opponent. I am glad to assure you that your brother does not join his army. Tomorrow we head for Flodden Field where we shall see them off…

One thing I should tell you clearly. I have made a will, in case things should go badly here. I have named you guardian of our living son. This will surprise no-one. I have also named you Regent. There will be uproar; my Lords in Council will dispute a female Regent, but I wish it in recognition of your devotion to the children and your good judgement. I do not know another way to secure our children's safety. I find myself acting in these contrary ways, tangled in a mess of thought. What I desire above everything is to hurl myself into the fight. It's a kind of cleansing. Women can't understand this…

When I return I shall begin preparations for my crusade. I want you to display the purple silk hat and the jewelled sword the Pope sent me; it will inspire the people. I try not to feel false pride but my heart swells, Margaret. To be named 'Protector of the Christian Religion' is a great honour. I will need your optimism, your faith in me, to accomplish what I must do.

The light is going now. I will send this by a horseman. When you read it, likely the battle will be over and I will be on my way home.

Your most earnest and true love,

Jamie

Linlithgow. September 1513

My dear Jamie,

Little James is well. Our new child quickens already. I pray you shall christen him yourself in April before you attempt your crusade. That was a mighty quarrel we had before you left, My Lord. I would not have dared to speak so strongly but for defending our children's future. What folly if my brother, your enemy, should be the agent of our ruin. Whatever our deeds in life, it is our children, then theirs, who live on. I do not want either of us to be the cauterised stump of a family.

I came across a pair of our musicians last evening, arguing about what use they might be to you on the battlefield. I boxed their ears and sent them on their way, but I know that they would give their lives for you, as I would, if necessary.

Janet has departed north for good to Drummond's estate. I have let it be known that she will no longer be referred to as Janet BairArs at court. How may she become respectable if her past is not forgotten? I trust that she will now become as forgotten as all your other mistresses.

In time, dear Jamie, through all our trials we might come to real love...

Devotedly, your true wife,

Margaret

Jenny Wren

A Polish sailor had bitten a Southampton Wren's nipple off. Gasps and excitement rippled through the roomful of Wrens. They'd heard Poles were passionate but that was a bit much. They were still absorbing this piece of news when Daisy came back in carrying her bloomers over her arm. The Wrens looked up in anticipation and Daisy gave a thumbs-down and grimaced.

'Polishing' was all she said but everyone burst out laughing.

Her friend, Jenny, came over and hugged her. 'Never mind, it was a good try.'

Daisy hurled the bloomers across the room where they landed on top of a locker. 'And I'm freezing cold again.'

She threw herself on her bed and sighed. Most of her escapades ended like this. The first issue of uniform that arrived had contained packages of voluminous knitted bloomers, impossible to walk in without chafing thighs. Daisy had cut out the crutches, put her head through the hole, arms through the legs and worn hers as slightly lumpy jumpers under her jacket, until discovered by Petty Officer Raleigh.

Daisy said she'd rather do any amount of *polishing of pointless objects* – standard punishment for misbehaving Wrens – than have Raleigh give her one of her martyred looks. The seldom seen but saintly Raleigh, was terrifying in her cool manner and high expectation. Now Daisy had the look and the polishing to deal with. But not *confined to barracks*.

'Thank goodness for that at least,' she whispered to Jenny. 'I'm seeing Roy tonight.' She raised her voice to ask the room 'Who's got the nylons?'

The nylons were passed across the room, freshly washed and neatly folded. It was a rule kept as carefully as any Naval order. A girl with a date had first call on the nylons. Between the six of them someone would be able to replace them from time to time once the little dabs of nail varnish no longer stopped the ladders.

'Must be your turn soon, Jenny. When are you going to say yes to Bates?'

Jenny blushed and turned away, muttering. 'Not ever, he's married.'

'And a long way from home. Another date wouldn't hurt,' Daisy considered.

Jenny turned away to conceal her blush. She was still angry and hurt that Andy Bates had waited for weeks to tell her he was married, waited until he knew she was falling for him. At first just a dance partner, he had twice walked her back to barracks and the last time he had kissed her goodnight and she had kissed him back. Then he told her he was married, *just to be clear* he said, before trying to kiss her again. She had frozen.

'So what do you think I am?' she had blurted out. 'Some sort of tart!'

He'd started to explain. They'd married young, didn't really get on any more. He thought she had boyfriends when he was away. But he really liked Jenny, wished, oh how he wished, they'd met earlier. Couldn't she try to understand?

Jenny was up from the country, a little Devonshire village, where everyone knew everyone and lives unerringly followed well defined paths. In her first weeks as a Wren, her eyes and ears had been wide with astonishment as she met and mixed with girls from London whose jokes and vocabulary were as colourful as the men's. The idea of a married man dating a single girl had surprised her. She had been even more shocked to discover that the other Wrens weren't moved at all, only amused at her naivety.

Daisy had commented, 'Well, it's either masturbation or infidelity when they're far from home. And there's a war on.'

'That's no excuse,' Jenny had replied sharply. 'How can we make sense of fighting a war if our personal conduct is shoddy?'

Daisy hadn't heard her and Jenny was glad because, even to herself, she sounded stuffy. She didn't want Daisy to turn away from her and things had certainly changed in her world. After three years of war, three years of living and working away, the village had receded into an unreachable past. She thought it a real possibility that she might not want to return home at all.

Daisy was back late and had to climb in the bathroom window, swearing roundly when she snagged the precious nylons on the latch. A light went on down the hallway and a voice called out. She slipped into the dormitory to her bed, shoved the body shape of bed clothes that Jenny had rolled up to one side and slipped in beside them just before the door was flung open and a bright torch light panned the room.

'My, but some of us flourish on Navy grub. Getting quite fat. Report to me in the morning, Daisy Paine.' Leading Wren Beddoes, a personification of domestic and sartorial oppression, snapped into the silence.

Daisy would be in for more polishing.

When all was dark and quiet again, Daisy reached over to Jenny's bed and shook her.

'Are you awake?' she whispered fiercely.

Jenny rolled over, yawned and stretched. 'I am now.'

'Wake up – wake up! I have to tell you. I'm engaged! To Roy! Oh do wake up Jenny. I'm so excited.'

Jenny sat up. 'To Roy? You've only known him for three weeks.'

'I know. Isn't it romantic? He says why wait when there's a…'

'…war on. I know. But still, three weeks.'

'It's long enough to know that you're in love. And to show it.'

There was a silence whilst Jenny considered this. 'Oh Daisy – you didn't.'

'I did. We did. It was wonderful.'

'All the way?' Jenny fumbled for her torch and shone it on Daisy's face.

Her lipstick was smeared and she looked rather pale. There were streaks on one cheek.

'Have you been crying?' Jenny asked.

'Well, it hurt at first. We were standing up and he was very excited. I didn't quite know what to do so it was probably my fault. But we did it again and it was better.'

'Oh Daisy. Standing up? It sounds awful.'

'Better get changed. I'm a bit of a mess down there. Can't go to the bathroom in case Beddoes hears me. Have you a spare hanky?'

Jenny reached into her locker and pulled out a pile of hankies. Her Aunt Joan would not be pleased to think that the six fine lawn handkerchiefs, with a curling embroidered J in each corner, given as a birthday gift were to be handed over to her niece's friend to mop up the results of her immorality. Jenny could just hear her saying it but, since she suspected the hankies had been an unused gift to Joan passed on to Jenny, she handed the pile over to Daisy.

'Thanks. There's an awful lot of it.' Daisy rustled around in the dark, twisting to reach both sides of herself.

'I'll wash them,' she promised.

'Don't bother,' answered Jenny, shuddering. 'I take it, it wasn't quite the Valerie Hobson number?'

They both laughed, thinking back to the week before in the cinema when they'd sighed over Valerie Hobson's film romance, imagining themselves in Roger Livesey's strong arms somewhere in the Punjab.

'There weren't any sticky hankies in the film,' Jenny recalled, watching Daisy stash the rumpled pile in her locker.

'Don't suppose she made love in an alley beside the pub either – still, it was romantic, Jenny. He did say he loves me.' Daisy snuggled down and her voice became sleepy. 'Goodnight.'

'At least he's not married,' Jenny said, snuggling down too. 'Goodnight.'

There was a long enough silence for Jenny to close her eyes before Daisy murmured, 'Actually, he is.'

Daisy's creative way with uniform came into its own with her posting to Wren Despatch Rider – none of the others opted to change their smart uniforms for the hotchpotch appearance of a despatch rider in full kit, or the danger. Daisy's brother in the Fleet Air Arm had liberated a pair of flying boots so she didn't have to wear sea-boot stockings in wellingtons, but she had to make do with regulation breeches and gaiters and a jacket cut for a man, khaki and rubber-proofed, that hung down to her knees. In goggles and gauntlets she was an intimidating sight. The best thing about it was that she was excused most parades because she looked more like a man than a woman. Her work was the same, more like a man's than a woman's. Jenny's heart was in her mouth every time Daisy set off on a duty run, especially at night or when it was wet. She was often delivering or collecting from around the docks where the lighting was poor and the surfaces slippery. Twice she had carried cases of live ammunition between bases and once ran into a parked car in the blackout, spilling herself and her motorbike across a harbour square in a shower of sparks before coming to a bruising halt against an unlit lamp post. Jenny admired and worried in equal measure but Daisy was jubilant, loving the risks.

'Nothing's ever going to be the same again,' Andy said.

Jenny half pushed him away, furious with herself for letting him walk her back to barracks again. She knew what was coming. 'I thought it was what we were fighting a war for, to save our way of life.'

'You can't put the genie back in the bottle, Jenny. Don't you think it's better this way? More grown up?'

They had spent the last few hours discussing their relationship. He was so willing to reason it out and part of Jenny longed for a sweeping away of reason in a torrent of passion, but she didn't want to go against the rules. He could have gone after one of the others. Few of them objected to going all the way. Daisy liked to say fucking which sent a horrified thrill round the room, but only Jenny and a vicar's daughter hadn't joined the club. Sometimes, listening to their sexy talk at night, Jenny felt the pangs in her groin and knew she would like it too. In the day, at work, she often convinced herself that Andy was right, they couldn't predict what would happen next week, let alone next year or forever, so to take their happiness was justifiable. Two girls had lost their men already, one missing in action, one dead. Jenny had gone on seeing Andy, telling herself that she could enjoy their friendship without going all the way. He went along with it, never leaving her in any doubt that he wanted her sexually, and worse, that he knew that she wanted him. And he loved her.

'It's not just about today. Chances are all three of us will survive this war. What then?'

'We'll be changed. Strangers in our old lives. She wants a divorce.'

Jenny stood very still.

'She wrote. She's in love with a butcher.' His voice was dull. 'Says he's willing to be the guilty party. She wants it as soon as possible. She's pregnant.'

If he was sad he didn't show it. Perhaps any rejection is hurtful, she thought, maybe he was thinking of the time when they had been so much in love they had married too soon.

'Mind you, that's what she told me. That she was pregnant,' Andy added.

'And wasn't she?'

'She *said* she had a miscarriage. I don't know, do I? She spent the afternoon in bed and was at the pub in the evening.'

35

Jenny couldn't imagine such a thing. 'That's awful, Andy. I'm so sorry.'

So, under a sycamore tree in the park, Jenny went all the way with Andy, giving comfort and love as best she could. She was a little embarrassed when he paused to pull on a condom. She looked up through the fretwork of branches. She was disappointed that they could bare so little and muffled a squeal when he pushed into her. He said her name over and over and she felt the flushing of her whole body in response to that rather than the urgency of his thrust. She felt his focus wholly on her and it thrilled her. Afterwards he was as tender as she could have wished, touched that she had been a virgin – girls always claim they are, he said – and she was momentarily stung that he hadn't taken her word for it. Their slow walk back to the barracks was as a new conspirators. She slept very deeply.

'Shit!'

Jenny woke up quickly. Daisy was on the edge of her bed, head down over a bowl, dribbling and spitting.

'What's up?'

'What's it look like? I'm being sick.'

'Bad luck. What did you eat last night? I thought the sausages were a bit off.'

'Not that kind of sick. It's the one that goes with a late monthly. Shit!'

'Daisy – really?'

'Yes, really – too much of a good thing.'

'And you didn't...?'

'He doesn't like them – says it's like hammering with a rubber…oh, bugger!' Daisy started to cry.

A few weeks later Daisy asked if they could take a long weekend's leave together. An aunt had a cottage they could stay in while she was away. Jenny said yes, hoping that the increasingly jittery Daisy might talk and calm down. They had hardly spoken since Daisy's announcement. Daisy had a dispatch to see to on the Friday morning but Jenny could make her own way to the cottage-and Daisy would get there as soon as she could. In the event it was nearly 9.00 p.m before a very anxious Jenny heard the taxi and opened the door to her friend. In the dim hall light Jenny thought Daisy looked very pale. They drank the hot chocolate that Jenny offered, then Daisy claimed tiredness. It had been a long bike run that morning and the taxi had made her feel sick. They would talk in the morning, she promised.

Jenny woke up quickly, sensing distress. She crossed the landing and opened the bedroom door. Daisy was rolling in her bed groaning, clutching her belly and sweating. Jenny pulled back the covers.

'I'll get the doctor.'

'No don't. It'll pass,' Daisy hissed through her teeth.

'But Daisy, it might be a miscarriage.'

'Hope so. That's the idea.' Daisy groaned on the crest of something. 'Just run me a bath, can you?'

'I'd rather get the doctor.'

'You'll get me arrested. Just run the bloody bath, will you!'

Jenny ran the bath all the while listening to Daisy's low moaning.

It took all morning. Daisy lay in the bath weeping, sweating and swearing by turns. Jenny wiped away the sweat and tears and chattered over the swearing, topping up the hot water when Daisy started to shiver. A rush of blood in the water and Daisy heaved like a seal, then lay so still that Jenny thought she had just witnessed her friend's death.

'I think that's the worst of it now.' Daisy's voice was very small. She looked doll-like in the pink bathwater, her head lolling over the side, eyes shut. 'Thanks.'

Jenny never knew how she managed hours afterwards. Helping Daisy out of the bath, wrapping her in towels. Draining the bath and its debris. Running a fresh bath, lighting the fire in the sitting room, making hot sweet tea, taking blankets and pillow to the sofa. She did not allow her feelings to connect with the situation. She did what she thought would be best for Daisy.

In the bathroom Daisy was soaping her arms. 'That was a rotten thing to do to you,' she said.

'We'll talk later. It's warm in the sitting room. Are you ready to come through?'

Wrapped in blankets beside the fire, sipping tea, Daisy recovered some colour. Jenny busied herself in the tiny kitchen making a cottage pie, unwilling to trust herself to say anything level. Anger, anxiety, concern and elation surged through her head. Every time she looked at Daisy she wanted to hit her or hug her. In the end she handed her a plate of cottage pie and a fork and sat beside her with another. They were both hungry.

'I should have told you. But I was afraid you wouldn't come.'

'Couldn't Roy have come?'

'He's on leave. Gone home to ask his wife for a divorce.'

'Will she agree?'

'*Everybody's doing it…*' Daisy sang weakly. 'I don't know.'

'Is that what you want?'

'I don't know that either.'

'Oh Daisy. All this for something you're not sure of.'

'Actually, I did it for my bike.'

After their laughter had subsided, in the hug that followed, Jenny checked Daisy's body temperature against her own in case she was delirious.

Daisy was suddenly serious again. 'It's the most important thing in my life.'

'Your bike?'

'I don't have to be a girl on my bike. I'm free.'

'But it's work.'

'I can't explain, Jenny. It's like the sex. We're so used to behaving we don't question anything. We just behave.'

'Like you just have?'

'I didn't say it was all wonderful. It isn't much fun biking through the blackout or filthy weather. I get scared. Some of the sailors are beasts on the quiet. You try being a girl delivering a message at midnight to an officer on his own in a hut. Grim. But when it's just me on the road, thinking my own thoughts, doing something more important than typing in the office, I feel free.'

'It's *quite* important your precious messages get typed.'

'I don't mean you *just* type. I'm sure everyone's doing vital work but, let's face it, not many of you would want to do my job. You wouldn't, little mouse. But it's me.'

'So was this. Are you going to tell me about it?'

'Not right now.'

'You'll need a proper check-up.'

'Can't do that. Doctor would report it. I'll be all right. I'm basically healthy.'

'But…'

'Oh shut up, Jenny. Look, it's done with. No, sorry, shouldn't have said that…but lots of women miscarry without medical help.'

'Maybe, but not the help you've had. Daisy, you could have died.'

'I know.'

Daisy wept softly until at last she fell asleep on the sofa. Jenny tucked her up under the blankets from her bed, wondering if her flushed face was from lying all evening near the fire or the first sign of infection, and what she would do if it was. They wouldn't be able to approach the MO. Daisy would be dismissed from the service straight away and no doctor would treat her without reporting her condition. Jenny found herself thinking *one of the nurses perhaps* and then was horrified knowing what trouble they would all be in, and all through Daisy's rash actions. She would already be for it if anyone found out about this weekend at the cottage, *aiding and abetting*, and what Daisy's aunt would make of her home being used for such a purpose, she shuddered to think. With this thought in mind Jenny went back to the bathroom with a bucket of hot soapy water, a scrubbing brush, cloths and a mop and scrubbed until she was sweating. She found a can of

Jeyes Fluid which she poured down all the plugholes and the toilet, trusting that its distinctive smell would go overnight. From time to time she looked in on Daisy who was breathing softly in her sleep – *lucky you, Daisy* – Jenny whispered in passing. Just another day before they would have to return to barracks with Daisy ready to get right back on her bike. It was understood that dispatch riders made no claims for time out of the saddle because they were women. Jenny crossed her fingers.

'That was decent of you,' Andy commented.

'I didn't really have a choice. She didn't tell me before she got there.'

'You could have left her. Come back,' he said.

'She's my friend. How could I have done that?'

'You're sweet. That's why I love you.'

'Well, that was a fortnight ago and she seems well enough. We haven't really spoken about it. I don't think she wants to.'

'She doesn't waste any time, she's seeing Greg Someone, another despatch rider, another married man.'

'That'll be why she's avoiding me.'

'You're her friend, make sure she gets herself some rubbers this time.'

'It's all a bit sordid, isn't it? Not quite how we dreamed of love.'

'That was before. This is better than a dream, it's real. Not perfect, but once the divorce is through we can marry and, after the war…'

Jenny shut him up with kisses.

In the end Jenny attended the funeral with three other Wrens and Daisy's parents. Andy was on duty and Greg was 'busy' – he didn't say what with.

Daisy had been rushing back through the dark and wet to be with Greg, looking forward to being enveloped in one of his great bear hugs. The pain in her lower back she had put down to the day's work, three two-way deliveries, mostly in rain mixed with sleet. She had thought it would ease when she got off the bike or, what a nuisance!, that it was her first returning period after that business. Greg wouldn't mind. They could just talk. Perhaps about the future. About after the war. When a particularly sharp pang had made her stiffen in the saddle, she had felt the wheel start to slide and saw the twin hooded lights of a lorry just too late to control the bike's trajectory. She and it slid spinning under the wheels of the three-tonner and both were crushed, Daisy so broken that the MO could only shake his head at the carnage. He could not distinguish the signs of recent miscarriage in the mess of Daisy's broken bones. The report said *Traffic accident whilst on duty due to adverse weather and light conditions*. Petty Officer Raleigh delivered a short, well-informed evaluation of Daisy's time under her command and the four Wrens wept, Jenny with feelings she could not share.

'This is quite a decision.'

'Yes, M'am.'

'Are you sure about this?' Petty Officer Raleigh paused in her reading and looked hard at Jenny.

'Yes, M'am.'

'Is this because of Daisy?'

'No, M'am.'

'Because it was just an awful accident.'

'Yes, M'am.'

'Very well, be careful and Good Luck.'

'Yes, M'am.'

'Dismissed.'

In her greatcoat and goggles her small frame was overwhelmed. Jenny stood by Daisy's grave and told her about the training, the times she'd been scared, when she'd nearly given up. She'd written the application and begged Daisy's flying boots from her family. She'd determined to stop being Daisy's *little mouse*. The bike and boots were too big for her, she hated the petrol reek that permeated her clothes and she still feared each outing might be her last. She might not marry Andy, she might never go home, she might be killed in a bombing raid but Jenny promised Daisy she would live in the moment until after the war.

She turned away and pulled her gauntlets on.

'Thanks, Daisy.'

Point Of Principle

Verity arrived early so she could think. She laid out twenty-one chairs in curved lines, three rows of seven, each row offset in front of the line behind so that everyone could be seen from the Chair. There was a good chance of a full attendance. When she'd e-mailed the agenda, including a discussion point, most of the local members had e-mailed back to say they'd be there. Rosie, their newest member, had asked for the discussion. Rosie was young, not long out of university, with a flush of red hair down to her shoulders and pale skin. She looked like a pre-Raphaelite painting and said she was a feminist. She had joined the group three months ago, spoken several times at meetings with wit and sharp questions. Not everyone appreciated her as Verity did.

She often thought their group was treading water, getting older and less passionate as illness, ageing, retirement and grandchildren occupied their thoughts. When was the last time I did something? she asked herself. Rosie's gauche question – *How do I know I'm a pacifist?* – kept her awake all week, glad that something other than petitions and letters to governments would be dealt with at the meeting. She was filling the urn when the sound of the door opening made her look up. Rosie walked down the hall towards her.

'You're early – half an hour to go yet,' Verity said.

'I know. I wanted to talk to you before the meeting.' Rosie slipped into a chair.

Verity gave her a close look. 'Something wrong? I'd say you were a bit paler than usual. Feeling nervous about tonight?'

Rosie looked up and Verity could see she'd been crying.

'Serves me right for trying to be too clever,' Rosie sniffed. 'Some discussion!'

Verity sat beside her, taking one of her hands and squeezing it. 'I think you'd better start at the beginning. Come on, out with it.'

Rosie took a deep breath, shuddered, then spoke. 'It's Mum's boyfriend. He's been around for six months but he moved in two weeks ago. I don't mind that. Mum was more cheerful than she's been since Dad died. That was four years ago. Started to buy clothes, got her hair cut, new makeup, you know. Yesterday was her birthday so I took her breakfast on a tray. She didn't answer the door when I knocked so I went in. She was under the covers, all of her, right up to her head. She told me to go away and I was cross. So I pulled the covers off her. She had two black eyes. Then he came in out of the shower. Said not to worry about her. She likes it, he said. He was wearing my Dad's bathrobe.'

Verity's breath hissed through her teeth.

Rosie shuddered. 'I wanted to kill him. Just take the knife off the tray and kill him.'

Verity put her arms round Rosie. 'First reaction, pet, you're bound to feel like that. What did you do?'

'Just fled.'

'How is your mum?'

'That's what's making me mad. She said it was a mistake. That he didn't mean it. One black eye maybe – but two, no way. I'm quite, quite sure she doesn't like it. She was ashamed. Dad was such a gentle person. Oh hell, Verity, I really want to kill him.'

Rosie was crying again but shook her head furiously. 'So I'm not a pacifist – answered my own dumb question, haven't I?'

Verity shook her head. 'It's not as simple as that, Rosie. I've lost track of the number of times I've thought the world would be better off without one so-and-so or another. It's not the desire to kill that denies your pacifism – denying the action confirms it though. The really difficult bit is yet to come. Getting her out of it.'

'She's avoiding me,' Rosie said.

Verity glanced at her watch. 'The others will be here very soon – why don't you slip away and we'll meet later at The General, the back room is usually quiet – there's a folk band on at The Mermaid. The others will go there. About 9.30 p.m?'

Rosie nodded and sniffed, pulled her coat around her and murmured, 'Thanks Verity.'

Verity endured the meeting and the group's vociferous disappointment at the no-show of their fiery new member. Some of them had brought notes for the discussion and she knew their frustration at being denied a good argument spilled into unkindness. She insisted that the discussion be held over until Rosie could come, and distracted them with the wording of a new petition and an early tea-break. Finally, after all the washing up, she locked up and hurried on to The General.

At The General she found Rosie deep in conversation with a man, her face flushed, tossing her hair this way and that as she spoke. She might easily be flirting with him, Verity thought, though she knew who Rosie was speaking to and that she was, most certainly, not flirting with him. He was looking at Rosie as if she were a Mars Bar. In her hand was a half pint glass, half full. The man raised his hand as if to placate Rosie by patting her and Verity saw the fury rise in Rosie's eyes, saw the glass rise too. She stepped forward quickly.

'Hello Rosie. Sorry I'm a bit late.'

Rosie and the man fell apart to make space for her. Verity glared at him.

He tipped his forelock to both of them and walked away.

'And that was…?' Verity asked.

'Him. My mother's boyfriend. Jake. Trying to get round me.'

'Hmm. Certainly thinks he's a charmer. Was he apologising?'

'Far from it – he was trying to tell me that my mum's menopausal, moody, provocative. He says she asks for it.'

'Was it just a coincidence – him being here?'

'No – I went back to the house for my heavier coat. He started to talk to me there, then he followed me. I didn't want to listen but he wouldn't shut up.'

'Where's your mum?'

'In her room, not letting me in.' Rosie was close to tears.

'Maybe you should come home with me tonight?' said Verity.

'What if he does it again?' Rosie asked. She shook her head emphatically. 'Thanks, but I need to look after Mum.'

'That might be more difficult than you think, if she's infatuated.'

'I'll get the police.'

47

'They can't do anything if she won't report it.'

'Well, fuck it – I'll take a knife to him!'

'You're back at square one, Rosie. No, come on, let's think this out. Shall I tell you what I did?'

It's still so vivid. His name was Will. He'd been nice too, at the start. My father died so my mother had the house. That's what Will was after. He had a salesman's charm and she was eating out of his hands right from the start. He charmed my younger brother and sister with sweets and little toys but I kept my distance and took nothing from him. I was the eldest and he could see I was suspicious of him. So he threatened me instead.

'You behave yourself or I'll get you put in a home. Don't think I can't. Your lovely mother will do anything I tell her to. You're just the type to benefit from some discipline. Bit out of hand since your Dad died, she says.'

All spoken softly with a smile. It was bad enough I couldn't be absolutely certain he wouldn't do it, but the worst bit was knowing my mother had said I was *out of hand*.

I knew I had been difficult, full of inexpressible anger and pain at Dad's sudden death when there were so many plans we had made which were stumped on the spot. A heart attack at fifty-seven. Mum had needed my help with the younger ones, who didn't understand either. In the absence of a close friend Mum loaded her own grief onto me, making me go through his wardrobe because she couldn't bear to do it, not noticing that I couldn't bear handling the pipe and Old Spice scented clothes either. Mum sat on the bed, flipping through a photo album, telling tearful anecdotes while I held my nose and stuffed clothes into black plastic bags. I felt cross that I'd been dragged into a caring role for her. I lost my temper a few times, especially when I felt weighed down with domestic tasks so late into the evening I couldn't do my homework properly. School had been the only thing that had continuity – at school I was still thirteen years old in Class 2A – not responsible for anyone but myself.

The first time I saw Mum injured I believed her explanation. There was a loose edge on the stair carpet (Dad would have fixed it) and I'd tripped on it once or twice. That's what she said she did.

'How did you bruise your face though – didn't you put your arms out to stop yourself?' I asked her, but Will was there and told me, sharply, to leave Mum alone and go and get the tea made. Then he knelt down beside Mum and whispered to her, something urgent rather than tender, stroking her knees all the while. After I'd fixed the tea I went to the shed and picked up Dad's hammer and some tacks. I stamped upstairs, knelt and banged many more tacks than necessary all round the loose carpet.

Suddenly he was there, standing over me, smiling. 'You're not to worry over your mother. I'll take care of her. She needs a man.'

I couldn't help myself. 'Then she'd better start looking, hadn't she?'

He went rigid. I saw his leg stiffen as if to kick. 'You could go down them too, you cheeky cow!'

I could see he didn't care whether I knew or not and just as surely I knew it wasn't the first time he'd hurt Mum. I stood to face him. I was on the top step, the stairs behind me. My grip on the hammer grew tighter, my knuckles were white. Something flickered in his eyes, doubt or fear, I didn't know. At the moment I knew I could strike him, I knew I wouldn't. If he'd pushed me, I would have fallen but he had lost his nerve, or thought better of having to explain two people falling down a flight of stairs on the same day, especially when the carpet had been nailed down between times. A pause. He swore and went past me in a gust of tobacco and sweat, slamming the front door.

'Mum?'

I'd taken in another cup of tea. Mum was sitting on the edge of her bed staring towards the window, dry-eyed but broken. She didn't raise her eyes.

'Mum, come on. Talk to me.'

She took the tea from me. 'Had your tea?' she faltered.

'No. I want to talk to you. Did you tell him I was out of hand?'

Mum shuffled on the bed. 'I might have. I don't know. You were shouting a lot. Maybe.'

'And did you think he might be a good person to deal with me?'

'I just needed some help. Without your Dad...'

'We're all without Dad. But we don't need him.'

'I can't do it on my own, Verity.' She started to cry quietly, still not looking up.

'Then I'll help. I'm not a child, not a small one anyway.'

'But the school...'

'Why don't I have flu for the next fortnight? We could make a plan for the cooking and cleaning. Get a routine going.'

Then she was really crying and I felt helpless in the face of such grief and shame and need.

'That's awful! What happened?' Rosie's eyes were wide with concern.

'Nothing. Everything. He just didn't come back. I heard later that he'd wormed his way into another widow's life, a childless one this time, just weeks after he left us.'

'And your mum?'

'She cried a lot at first. I did take the fortnight off and we got started on organising things. We couldn't tell the school in case they called in Social Services but I knew I could catch up a fortnight's work. Mum said I'd been brave but I didn't accept that. She meant standing up to him with a hammer in my hand and I couldn't get her to see that, if I was brave, it was in trusting myself not to hit him and not to give in to him either. In the end I was too much bother.'

Rosie was quiet for a while. 'So you think I should stand up to Jake, face him down? He's pretty nasty, you know.' She looked doubtful.

'I didn't say it would be easy. But if your mum can't do it… It's no good trying to get shot of him with force. That's how the cycle continues. It endorses his behaviour. You have to believe that somewhere inside he knows his relationship with your mum is based on fear. You have to behave better than he does. Hold up a mirror to him.'

'Not the police then?'

'Same sort of thing really. Someone making him behave. And if your mum won't press charges…'

There was a very long silence.

'OK,' said Rosie.

51

Verity laid out twenty-one chairs early so she could think. Silence all week but on her phone five minutes ago was the text from Rosie.

Change discussion point to How I Know I am a Pacifist R.

Not so provocative perhaps, but sure to generate a heated debate. Verity licked a finger and stroked a number one in the air.

In Context

She waited a week before she came to the graveside, long enough to be sure of being the only one there. She carried a creased heavy metal poster and a studded leather bracelet. Flowers, about to droop, speckled the ground in front of the headstone. She kicked the flowers away and placed her offerings tenderly in their place. She sang the chorus of *We are the Champions* in a wavering soprano. A passing dog paused, whined at her and she began to howl. The dog joined in as if he'd known him too. How they had howled together at gigs. Wolf had been such a nutter, looking for post-gig chances of a fight where he could jerk his forehead onto someone's nose. Those were the days. Those were the days before he had joined up one bored Saturday, before he went away and came back shorn and excited by the prospect of legal weaponry. Those were the days before he was posted, the days before he found himself in a sandy hell, building a reputation as a bit of a maverick, a hell-raiser, a wild card. All those things short-handed to *brave,* now that he was dead, blown to hundreds of hot pieces in a final explosion. She left off howling and knelt close to the earth.

'You wasn't doing your duty, was you, Wolf? You was still giving them the finger, wasn't you?'

She looked at the dog. No collar, skinny, wary.

'Want to come home with me? Wolf?'

Poppies

I will calm down.

And I will apologise, yes, before the police come.

Is he OK? I didn't hit him very hard, you know.

Yes, I know I shouldn't have hit him at all.

I'll pick up all the poppies, and pay for them.

I was trying to explain about my white poppy.

He wouldn't listen, that's why I hit him.

Very inappropriate, I agree.

He kept telling me it should be a red poppy.

He just wouldn't listen.

I have stopped crying. Yes, alright, I'll sit down here.

You could get me a cup of tea while we're waiting.

Why should I explain to you?

You a Samaritan or something?

No, I'm not getting agitated again – just had a bellyful of bullshit.

About my boy.

My dead boy.

I've heard it all – *my country right or wrong*.

The glorious dead, whether they were glorious or not.

Our brave boys, the same.

Don't talk to me about red poppies.

No, I know you didn't, but just in case you did.

You will listen…?

You live down the road from me, don't you? You know that gang of lads that hangs around the chippie, kicking bins and cursing, if they were suddenly to be transported to Iraq or Afghanistan, you'd be pleased as punch with their nerve.

The bullies among them would get to be corporals and the really nasty ones, sergeants. And if any of them came home via Wootton Bassett – that's *Royal* Wootton Bassett these days, though they've stopped the funerals – you can bet your boots you'll be waving a Union Jack for your local boy as tearfully as any of them.

I know they're decent boys, some of them. Come from good families like yours and mine, but when they went to war, when we sent them to war, they surely knew there was a good chance they'd be killed or injured? Did they think it was some sort of game? Was it the dead-end jobs round here? Or some army bullshit down at the pub?

Is it just human nature?

You know when you have a baby. And it's sleeping in the pram and you have that moment when you think there never was a better baby – do you remember the first time you thought perhaps he wasn't quite perfect after all? When you saw your two-year old swing a bat at another toddler with all its pathetic might, but determined on annihilation? Or a bunch of six-year olds turn on one of their group because they've got different shoes or plaits and, day after day, make them feel small and frightened and alone. How does a child react to this? Suddenly discover the thing inside that says *pass it on*? The thing in you that says you can kill. Just a bit developed, nurtured with soft words to do hard things. What is it you say to a young man, basically decent, that convinces him that he's allowed to kill another person that he doesn't even know?

I had two sons. One dead, one still in the army. Rob and Jimmy. Nothing special except to me. Rob was killed a year ago, a land mine. Just him. Stood on it, just like he did at home, always falling over things. He didn't have time to kill anybody. So, no hero's welcome home. Just a bag with his personal things in it. Photo of a girl I hadn't met, pretty girl, says Manchester on the back so fairly local, and his AC/DC fag case (bit dented) and three unposted postcards, only one of them addressed. It was for me asking for more cotton-rich socks. He has – had – awful feet, Rob, and found these cotton-rich socks were a help. He's written it very carefully so I could see what he wanted – cotton-rich socks in his awful handwriting but big and loopy so I could read it. I didn't sleep properly for nearly a year. The doctor offered me tablets but it was at night I could see Rob's face the clearest so I refused them. I just caught up sleep in the day. Lost my job and my husband, Larry. I reckon he was looking for the excuse, but I gave it to him. Got a bit slack on the cooking and housework, didn't fancy sex anymore. But he wasn't a talker, never said a word to me about Rob. I don't know if he spoke to anyone else. Down the pub maybe, with the other men. I wasn't glad he went but I was glad not to have to think about him too. Jimmy's trying to get him to come back. Larry's staying with his sister, Irene.

Jimmy talks to me a bit. He's careful not to worry me with details. I want to beg him to leave the army, to come home and look after me and mourn his little brother, but it won't work. That thing they do in the army where they can make you do bad things also works on your family. You can lock them out so the natural things, like keeping you from harm, seem like an imposition. It goes in with the haircut. Jimmy has his hair cut so short it feels like bristles. I hate it. I remember his baby soft hair that grew into ringlets before he went to school, and even after, it was never shaved until he joined up. When he came home that first weekend I didn't recognize him.

Sometimes I try to talk to him, just a little, about the army. He gets angry. He doesn't understand why I want to know. He likes me to remember Rob as he was, not start asking about their lives out there. I tell him, I had a dad of my own in the Navy, I know about shore leave in foreign places. I won't be shocked. But I will, Mum, he says. I don't want to tell you all that stuff. I want you thinking of me working hard and doing my duty. I want you to be proud of me. He won't say any more so it's like being with Larry, like having the attic full of stuff you want to get out and there's no key for the padlock. Who do they talk to, the soldiers, when they're frightened or lonely?

I'm not proud. I'm just frightened.

I think about the other mothers a lot, the *enemy* mothers. They must grieve the same. They must wonder how all this hell descended on their lives out of the blue. They must wonder why their precious sons have been sent to risk their bodies fighting invaders whose purpose they don't understand. Their sons who mended cars and made bread and courted girls in the villages have gone away in trucks waving weapons above their heads. Their fear is like mine, that they will not see their sons again. Or that their sons will return stone-hearted, stone-headed.

Hence the white poppy. It's for all of them, the soldiers and the civilians, all dead as a result of war. It's what I feel. I think if you only remember your own dead, you're taking the side of those who decide for war.

It's so hard to see the right of it.

There's so much propaganda, so much spin. Did you notice Poppy Day getting like Christmas this year? All over the BBC for weeks, every presenter, every programme. It's supposed to be two minutes at the eleventh hour of the eleventh day, or a church service and a bit of a march around.

It'll be a reality show next, you wait and see.

What if, before a war is declared, to show good faith, the politicians agree to sacrifice a son each, knowing that any such war will take the lives of the sons of thousands of families?

These thoughts go round and round in my head – all the ways it's wrong to send our best beautiful boys to be ripped apart. I saw a newsreel last week, footage from Iraq of an army chaplain leading a service. There wasn't a soundtrack but I would like to know how a Christian minister inspires young soldiers, and they are so young, to follow orders to kill. I remember a clip from way back from the Vietnam war – an American padre blessing bombers before they set off. I wanted to know what he said too.

Just this week I heard about a schoolboy put out of a church service for wearing a white poppy. By the minister.

It seems easier to understand when life was more physical, when you had to hunt, compete for food or shelter or even when men fought hand to hand. If you had to look at someone's face when you were shooting him or stabbing him, would you be less willing to do it? Or more aware of what you were doing? Seems to me that every move away from the physical is a move away from being responsible. Or moral perhaps. Jimmy did tell me they can't see the people they're firing at. Their weapons spray rounds. So I suppose they hit women or children or animals quite often. I can't imagine that. Being shot at in your own town, your own home. Would I want a red poppy then? Would fear make me vengeful?

I used to wear a red poppy like everyone else, before my boys signed up, before Rob was killed. I didn't really think about it, I just did it. The sight of marching soldiers on Remembrance Day, the slow sad music and the old soldiers standing as straight as they could made me feel proud too. As did those films —*The Dam Busters*, *633 Squadron*, *The Bridge over the River Kwai* – and others, with their granite faced heroes all on the side of right. I never thought of who drowned in the floods from the broken dams, who were crushed by the falling rocks or fell from the train on the bridge. The start of my questions came after seeing *The Longest Day*. It was about D-Day but showed what happened to the Americans, French and Germans too, and there weren't really any gung-ho heroes. But you have to think of the other side as villains or the whole thing becomes unbearable. I couldn't watch the later films. I walked out of *Born on the 4th July* and haven't been to one since. My dad said, why on earth do you want a war film to be realistic? but he'd been in the Navy and seen some awful things. Not that he talked about it but he did wear a red poppy.

Do you want me to shut up now? No? My heart's thumping and I'm short of breath. I'm not ill, just feeling. I haven't spoken to anyone like this before. Haven't felt like this either. Maybe thumping that poppy seller unblocked all the feeling. I didn't know I felt all these things. Maybe I should tell more people.

Did you call the police? There's one talking to the poppy seller. Will they arrest me, do you think? I will say sorry to him, for hitting him, not for what I said. Now all I have to do is get someone to listen...

Three Minds

She couldn't help herself. As soon as she turned into the
street, Maisie accelerated in case her mother was watching
from the window. Most days Chrissy would time her only by
the clock on the wall and she probably wouldn't say anything
today of all days, but she'd know how many minutes her
three mile run had taken. She would know whether it was
longer or shorter or the same as yesterday, the day before and
the day before that. Some days Chrissy would be holding a
stopwatch. Maisie never lost the feeling of incongruity at the
sight of her mother, dressed from head to toe in flowing
clothes, holding and using an electronic stopwatch. As she
leapt the final three concrete stairs the front door was flung
open.

'Good time, Maisie – come on in. I've made us a birthday
breakfast.' Chrissy hugged her sweat-soaked daughter,
enjoying the warmth that flooded from Maisie's body to hers.

Maisie wriggled in her arms. There were damp patches all
down her mother's linen tunic. 'Thanks, Mum. I'll grab a
quick shower, then breakfast. Is Grandad down yet?'

'Not yet. Give us a kiss then – you're not too old for that,
I hope,' Chrissy laughed.

'I'm smelly! Let me go.' Maisie wriggled harder and
pulled away.

Chrissy's face fell momentarily but she was distracted by
the postman arriving with an armful of white envelopes.

Maisie escaped through the door and ran upstairs.

Chrissy shuffled the envelopes. There was one brown
envelope addressed to Maisie among the birthday cards,
postmarked Canadian Light Infantry. She frowned then

remembered the project Maisie was doing. Something to do with the woman soldier that Maisie idolised. Photographs and news clippings were pinned all over Maisie's bedroom. Nichola Goddard.

Other girls went for rock or movie stars, but not my daughter, she has to pick a serving combat soldier who happened to be a woman. And happens to be dead. Chrissy thought of her own teenage pin-ups – Che, Tariq, Lenin, Gandhi – and headed indoors.

Breakfast took ages that morning. There were parcels to open, cards to read and laugh over. Dougie shared his granddaughter's pleasure. After each card was read he arranged them on the mantlepiece. Chrissy did not see Maisie conceal the brown envelope but noticed that it wasn't among the detritus on the table.

Something private then.

Once she'd put the second cafetière on the table, there was a quiet moment when Maisie seemed to be waiting for something. The silence became uncomfortable.

Finally she said, a little embarrassed, 'What about you two?'

They laughed and Chrissy reached into her own pocket and took out an envelope. 'With my love.' She handed it to Maisie.

There was a rip then Maisie gasped. 'Oh Mum, Business Class. They must have cost a fortune!'

'Well, long plane flights can be a pain in Economy – it's twelve hours to Canada. And you'll only be eighteen once.'

Dougie produced his own envelope which contained an invitation for three to dine at Raymondo's, the most expensive restaurant in town, that night. Maisie wondered how many weeks of his pension that would cost and vowed to eat the cheapest things on the menu, but Dougie told her he'd arranged to have a menu without prices precisely to avoid that kind of nonsense.

'There are times to spend money,' he said, 'and this is one of them.'

Chrissy pulled one more package from under a cushion and pushed it, tentatively, across the table. 'Just this once,' she said.

Maisie didn't know what to say as she unfolded the delicate red fabric from its tissue wrapping. The looks on their faces stumped her. Dougie beaming, Chrissy wary but hopeful.

'It's very...pretty,' she said, making Dougie laugh.

'Pretty? It's bloody beautiful! You can't go to a place like that in trainers and trackies. I've had my suit cleaned specially.'

Chrissy said nothing, couldn't even look into Maisie's eyes while she sensed her indecision.

Maisie held the dress up. 'OK. Just this once.'

Maisie was puzzled, irresolute. The dress wasn't anything that Chrissy might have worn. Chrissy didn't like delicate clothes. She didn't wear strong colours and she definitely didn't like seductive. The dress was all three. Maisie stood in front of her mirror, having to peer around the press cuttings, and saw an unfamiliar self, a girl more physically like her mother than usual. What was plump in Chrissy was muscle in Maisie but they had the same basic generosity of curves, the same neat waist. She shook her hair loose and saw she looked even more like her mother. There was a photograph downstairs of Chrissy in jeans and duffle coat at some peace demo. They could have been twin sisters.

Better get on with it, then.

She went downstairs.

Chrissy's face was a picture when Maisie walked into the kitchen, a mixture of pride and trepidation. Maisie saw there were tears in her mother's eyes.

'I don't have tights or shoes, Mum – can I borrow your slip-ons?'

There followed a lot of women business, offers of make-up (just a little), a lower cut bra and an under-slip. This rare softness between them made Maisie brave.

'Why did you choose this particular dress, Mum?'

Chrissy mumbled something about wanting her to feel good, to look her best.

'But all the time I was a kid you never dressed me up like this.'

Chrissy looked at her tomboy daughter and said that Dougie would appreciate it. Finally he would have a beautiful granddaughter on the outside too.

'Is that what you feel? I thought the idea was that I would be free to be myself.'

Chrissy sighed. How to embark on this one without getting into one of those fierce confrontations that left them both raw? She could see Maisie rolling contradictory things around in her head. Change the subject? Diversionary tactic?

'That letter you got, with the Canadian Light Infantry postmark, anything I should know about?'

Maisie knew she had to tell but pleaded to leave it for a day. Have the birthday meal with both of them. Return to normal antagonisms tomorrow. But Chrissy's question had to be answered so Maisie asked her to sit down and brought her a herbal tea while she worked out a strategy for telling her mother something she most definitely would not want to hear.

'It's an application form.'

Chrissy raised her eyebrows. 'For what?'

'To join the Canadian Army.'

Chrissy's long pedigree in protest and peace work raised so many arguments she couldn't voice any of them.

Maisie talked quietly, about her admiration for Nichola Goddard, how her death in combat had ennobled her, made her truly equal to the men around her. How she had talked to Lucy...

Chrissy exploded. 'You discussed this with Lucy! My sister who you haven't seen since you were two years old. You talked to Lucy! Not to me!'

Maisie talked into the storm, explained that they'd e-mailed and skyped each other over the last month, as soon as Maisie knew she could go to Canada. Lucy, still in the family home in Canada, had been to a couple of the Goddard Memorial services and told her how highly regarded Nichola Goddard was.

'You talked with my sister about this crazy idea and not to me! When it's me that's paying for it.'

Maisie sighed. Why would she tell her mother when she reacted like this? Wasn't it always the same? Chrissy would defend any freedom except Maisie questioning her ideas.

Chrissy got up abruptly and raked in a drawer until she found what she wanted. She grabbed the plane tickets from the table and put the scissors to them. 'Give me one good reason.'

Maisie sucked in breath but stared her mother down. She spoke clearly. 'Because I'd go anyway. You always said I should do what I think is right.'

When Dougie came in from his walk he found Chrissy, still clutching the plane tickets, in a black temper in the living room and no sign of Maisie. Shared living had trained his instinct to detect the level of tension between them. It was high. When he touched her shoulder she began to cry, not a common occurrence.

'Trouble?'

She nodded and told him what had happened.

'I was in the Royal Navy. It wasn't so bad. The WRENs were great. I remember...'

Chrissy told him to shut up. It wasn't the same. Maisie wasn't going to be a bloody typist, she was talking about the infantry, she wanted to carry a gun, go to Afghanistan.

'Do they allow that?'

Chrissy knew they did, she had listened to Maisie's school presentation. Since 1980, Canadian women had been allowed into combat roles. Captain Nichola Kathleen Sarah Goddard was the first to die in combat. Maisie was half-Canadian and could join the Canadian Forces. She wanted to be like Nichola Goddard. Probably, she wanted to die like Nichola Goddard.

'Calm down, Chrissy – think back. Weren't you just the same? All those demos and protests. Your mother hardly slept a night through your teenage years. That night the police brought you home…'

Chrissy waved that away. How many times had she explained to him they did that on purpose, hoping to rile the parents enough to make them keep their kids in at night? Had they not been even a little proud that she had principles?

'Isn't that what Maisie's thinking? Lord knows, Chrissy, I can't imagine her as a soldier but I couldn't see what you were getting at either. We thought we'd won a war, made something, and then you and your friends wanted to break it all.'

His tired arguments fell on her deaf ears but she was surprised at his continuing vehemence.

That was so long ago, nothing like the torment she was feeling. She hadn't actually done anything back then. She'd been too scared for the illegal stuff. She'd just been a nuisance and a constant worry to her parents. This was not the same. Maisie, her lovely Maisie, at the start of her adult life with a fistful of Highers and a university place booked for a year ahead, could get herself killed on the back of a bout of hero-worship and heaven knows what support from an aunt she didn't even know.

'Lucy wouldn't give her bad advice. She's a teacher. She's always been steady.'

That had always hurt – the knowledge that her parents preferred Lucy who did well at school, had lots of sociable friends and no interest in politics. Good old teacher's pet, Lucy – Mummy and Daddy's favourite.

'We most certainly did not prefer Lucy! We loved you as much as you let us. She was easier than you, it's true, but we did what we thought was best for you. Even when it went against the grain. You could be as generous with Maisie – you could at least listen to her.'

It went on and on. The poking at old grudges and opinions not shared for years, father and daughter lacerating each other, listening even less than they had when it was all immediate. At some point it all petered out as both parties contracted into their own resentful thoughts. Dougie went off for a nap.

Chrissy made more tea, called out 'Tea's ready' but no-one came. It went cold in the pot. She went upstairs and fell into a restless sleep.

Around six o'clock, Maisie reappeared in tracksuit and trainers, hair tightly plaited, face scrubbed to a sheen. She carried the red dress to the table, took up the scissors and began to shred the fabric, running the blade from hem to waistline, through the bodice to the shoulder straps which she snipped off with a quick movement. She picked up the plane tickets from where Chrissie had dropped them and cut them up too. She piled the pieces of material and card on the table and sat down to wait. Around six-thirty a freshly scrubbed and suited Dougie came and stood beside her. She ran her fingers through the shreds in front of her.

'It's a kind of solution, Granddad – makes us equal. Equally pissed off. I'll earn the money to go to Canada and she'll let me go. Shall we wake her? She'll want to get changed before we go out.'

It was a lavish meal, superficial as their conversation, everything looked most carefully arranged for maximum effect from very little content. Maisie thought the spun-sugar nets on the desserts were particularly remarkable. Chrissy said the vegetarian option was better than some, mostly variations on cheese dishes, she had been offered elsewhere. Dougie cleared his plate with the end of a crusty roll as if he had been very hungry, declaring that jus was nearly as tasty as a good gravy. The silences that laced their conversation got longer and longer. Once, when Dougie reached across to steal a spoonful of cream from Maisie's dessert and she mimed shooting him with her thumb and forefinger, Chrissy seemed about to start something but thought better of it and looked away, rubbing something from her eyes.

They walked home each in their own dark.

Bags I Go First

About midday the sun broke through. By one o'clock the lawn was dry enough to send the little boys out to play. Even though he was a head smaller than Ollie, Jimmy took the lead. Through the window their mothers could see Jimmy's arms directing operations and Ollie rushing back and forth from the play room to the sandpit where Jimmy presided.

Jimmy's mother clucked her tongue and shook her head. 'He's so bossy!' she said, not without fondness.

'Ollie's very accommodating,' Ollie's mother responded. 'Very popular at playgroup. Always helping.'

'The thing is, Jimmy's so quick, he's always there before the others.'

'Ollie thinks about things.'

'You have to have leaders though. Even at playgroup.'

'Nature will out. That's true.'

The mothers made sandwiches and came back to the window. By then the little boys had made a kingdom around the old rhododendrons. Jimmy was strafing the sky with an old rolling pin, wearing a cloak of old blanket and a fireman's helmet while Ollie patrolled the perimeter armed with a red plastic hammer.

'Does Jimmy ever play with girls?'

'There aren't any in our street.'

'Ollie has a bit of a fan club at playgroup. He's so gentle. They like that.'

'Bit soft, do you mean?'

'As opposed to?'

'Well, proper boys.'

The little boys became bored and tired and hungry and abandoned their kingdom and came to look for their mothers. Finding them engaged in a shrieking argument in the living room, they watched for a while then Ollie picked up a plate of sandwiches and offered it to Jimmy.

'Your mum's a wimp,' Jimmy said, taking a sandwich.

'Yours is a bully,' Ollie responded, stuffing one too.

For a moment they stood looking at the two dishevelled, sweating women.

Then the little boys went to the playroom and worked some more on a thousand-piece jigsaw they had started earlier.

Apple Pie For The Major

She's left, I know she has. Two large suitcases and both boys hustled into the back of the car. Her hair in an unusually untidy French pleat. She very clearly wiped her eyes with the backs of both hands before she started the engine. I can see their drive from my front room window so I am not inventing this scenario. I had seen it coming.

I suppose it can be difficult to be the wife of a war hero. Though she is considered to be beautiful, and the two boys sweet. She had been the subject of a magazine spread called *They also serve* …a sort of patriotic piece in one of those glossy monthly rags, with lots of photos of their elegant home and her with the boys gazing at a photograph of him in uniform. The tabloids took her up, photographing her in short skirts and low cut jackets. One of them commented on *Clarrie's Cleavage* and that started weeks of angry letters about *dishonouring a hero's wife*. For a while, she had been the centre of attention but then he came home and put her nose out of joint, good and proper.

He was the real thing, you see. Major Donald Hamilton MC. Military Cross; *awarded in recognition of exemplary gallantry during active operations against the enemy on land.* Handsome, immaculately turned out, self-depreciating, a man who denied his own heroism, who had been decorated for saving the lives of three of his men under fire. A man who said, 'Anyone would have done the same.' The flashing cameras made him recoil but she clung to his arm and beamed into the lens, leaning a little forward so that a hint of cleavage showed. It was all over the tabloids the next day. He can't have liked that.

The village gave him a reception when he finally came home. I was not on the organising committee as such but was asked to be responsible for organising desserts. I have judged the home-baking section at the village show for years and was particularly pleased when he commented warmly on my traditional apple pie when we shook hands in the line-up. There were those who fell for the lemon meringue pie that the vicar's wife supplied, over-sweet on the top but with a lemon flinch lurking underneath. She flounced a little and blushed, actually half-curtsied to him but I could tell he was genuine in preferring my honest offering and modest response. It was not necessary for him to return for a second helping but he did. Neither did I imagine the look of fellow travellers that we briefly exchanged over the pie dish.

So I know what must be done next. He must realise that he does not have to bear this alone. I shall communicate my support without assuming an emotional contract we have not yet acknowledged.

I have a box of Father's rare Alderman apples, this autumn's harvest, lovingly wrapped in tissue in the dark of my pantry. Father planted the tree in our garden in Scotland in 1946 to mark the end of the war. He was twenty-six, and I was born ten years later. For years we ate its fruits but I only knew it was special when he was invited to register the tree by the Orange Pippin and Home Orchard Societies, in recognition of his orchard skills and commitment to traditional varieties of apple. This apple makes the most perfect of apple pies and these will be the last. Father died three days after storing this year's harvest. The box of apples was the only thing I wanted from the house. This amused my brother and sisters.

'Some legacy!' I heard them laugh as they squabbled over the spoils.

I heard their gate rattle. He was placing the wheelie-bins on the pavement, squaring them neatly in line with the kerbstones. I'm sure he looked up at my window. I thought he seemed wistful.

So to the kitchen. I arrange my work space. Even after the hundreds of pies and cakes I have made, I measure my ingredients down to the half-teaspoon of cinnamon and ground cloves. This is the only way to ensure success. I make the pastry in the traditional way – short-crust for pies – and put it into the fridge to rest. The Aldermans release their sweet musk to the air as I unwrap them, their satin skins glowing. Few people bother to handle apples with care but I line up the six chosen fruits to be certain they are equal one to the other, giving each a brief polish with my apron. I skin, core and quarter them, put them in a bowl and blanch them with boiling water, drain them then lay them out in the red stoneware pie dish. I sprinkle them with lemon juice. Mother said so they would not discolour but I don't know. I have never dared leave the lemon juice out. I do not want to risk discoloured apples. While the apples are still hot I add the sugar, spices, sultanas and a knob of butter, then let it cool. The smell is very good. Wholesome.

Not to be confused with wholefood. That perhaps has been my battle in life, my modest claim to heroism. My mother taught me to bake. Not just to bake but all the facts she knew of food with her being a grocer's daughter. Her father had provided the whole village with wholesome food before the supermarkets came, and gave talks all round the area in the 1960s on the whiteness and lightness of the Chorleywood loaf. He used to take a loaf of brown bread round with him to demonstrate the improvement, stressing the remarkable longevity of the white loaf. His little cucumber sandwiches, once the crusts were trimmed off, were the fluffiest, sweetest things in the world.

Until the 1970s that is. It's all backwards now.

Incomers came into the village about then, buying up cottages at low prices and forming cabals that bullied the village shop into stocking their food fads, mostly foreign, brown rice and pasta, tofu and yoghurt, lentils, all very brown looking which they called 'ethnic'. Perhaps people should eat what they like but within a year of coming they had infiltrated the fête committee and the WI and were asking for the categories in the annual show to be changed to include wholefoods. I didn't understand it even from their point of view. They were prone to causes, often very obscure and most often foreign. They seemed keen on peace in the world, yet they wanted to compete with the village population at the annual show, not in the least a peaceful operation, I can tell you. Some very military operations around that including sabotage, spying and lying (several Victoria sponge entries resembling the very good M&S one and not a few jam jars with tell-tale smears of label adhesive discernible to the trained eye).

I notice that the incomers stayed away from the village reception – it's well known that British soldiers dream of sweet pies and custard. The refreshments were all properly traditional, steaming steak-and-kidney pies, bacon-and-sausage casserole and a full array of sweetly delicious desserts. I am so glad we decided against including wholefoods, though it took quite a campaign to defend the traditional. In the end it was an appeal to patriotism that won the day. With a war on, even a foreign one, people see sense.

Time to take the pastry out of the fridge and turn the oven on. Shake the fruit to distribute the melted butter, sugar and spices then roll the pliable pastry over the top and press a fork round the edges, careful to taper the angle round the sharp part of the oval. A little pastry left for a sculpture on the top – usually an apple with a stalk and two leaves but I could make a heart, or two even, on this one. I don't dare. I don't want to seem forward. A rose then. A tapered strip of pastry rolled from thick end to thin and a neat detail, the upper edges turned back on themselves. A full blown one and a bud, two serrated leaves and a stem with thorns if I use my smallest sharp knife. There. Brush with beaten egg.

So beautiful I feel myself flush all over, something I have grown familiar with since I met him.

I had not thought this could happen to me at this stage of my life. I am fifty-five and probably a virgin. I lived here through the 1960s. It wasn't just London where Love Ruled. There was a blacksmith's son, Georgie, who was the last one to cause this feeling in me. His bare sweaty back over the anvil did it and we mucked about in summer fields, hence the *probably* a virgin. His interest in me faded with the arrival of a new barmaid and there had been no other suitable, available man in the village until now. It crosses my mind that it may not be love but disease that has made me suddenly aware of an ache in my sexual parts. That it comes when I see him or think of him could be coincidental so perhaps I should see the doctor sometime soon. But I won't. I am enjoying the sensation and wonder if it will become even more urgent if, when, things move on. It ought to be soon. He is forty-four and I still have intermittent periods.

The oven buzzer sounds. The smell is indescribable. I wish I could bottle it. I would use it as perfume. It smells of meadows and happiness. I wipe a single apple-juice tear from the side of the pie dish and inspect the pastry but it is golden and perfect, a fitting tribute to his courage. While it cools I change my dress and comb my hair. He will see me anew.

There's no-one about. I don't think about what I will say. I put the apple pie on the wall of the porch while I ring the bell. I hear his footfall, see his shadow through the frosted glass. I pick up the pie. He opens the door, looks surprised to see me there so soon.

'Oh, hello. Miss…Miss?'

'It's Mary.'

'Right. Mary. What can I do for you?' His glance slips to the pie.

'I thought you might be hungry.'

'What?'

'I thought you might be hungry.'

He does look puzzled.

'It's an apple pie. You said you liked it.'

He remembers, a light bulb moment. 'Oh yes, the reception. I did enjoy it. But really, there's no need…'

'I wanted to.'

'Right. Well, thank you. I'm sure we'll enjoy it for tea.'

'You don't have to pretend, Major. I saw them go.'

His face falls. 'You'd better come in. I could do with some company.'

He leads me into their lounge, puts the pie on the table, picks up a glass of whisky. 'Care to join me?'

I have never drunk whisky. I am a sweet-sherry-at-Christmas drinker. 'Just a small one.'

He pours a lady measure and hands it to me. I sip it. I am full of courage. 'I thought you might need me. I know you've had a rough time.'

'That's very kind.'

'I do so admire you. You're the kind of man this country needs.'

He puts down his drink, takes me in his arms and kisses me fiercely. I can feel the good red blood rushing through his body as he crushes me to him. He smells of aftershave and whisky. He is warm like a woollen blanket, tense as a greyhound.

'I can't wait – take your knickers off.'

What he actually says is, 'What the hell are you talking about?'

A car turns into the drive and she gets out with the shouting boys, who rush up to him. 'Daddy, Daddy!' hurling themselves into his arms.

She stands smiling at them then turns to me. 'Mary, isn't it? Is that one of your lovely apple pies – how kind,' she says,

78

taking the pie from my rigid hands. 'People have been so kind. It's so lovely now that the papers and the TV have gone away. Would you like to come in for a cup of tea? I could do with one... Oh Donald, could you bring the suitcases in?' she calls over her shoulder.

I re-run my little movie in my head. I smile at her while thinking of her husband's stiffness. Very military, very much at attention.

She takes my arm, chattering away about what a day she's had, washing machine broken down, an imminent holiday, a stack of washing, so she'd piled it all into suitcases to take to a friend's. Then, in the car, something in her eye making them stream. The boys on a school holiday, leaving Donald behind to finish the packing. Imagine, a war hero doing the packing. He's slipped a few heroic notches in the last few minutes.

I find myself in the lounge with a cup of tea in hand and a packet of biscuits hastily found. I am to call them Clarrie and Donald and she slips away to make tea while he makes awkward conversation with me. I make a request.

He rummages in a desk drawer and shows me his Military Cross – a silver cross with four crowns, a purple and white ribbon – and murmurs, 'Any one of my Command could have had it.'

I protest. 'Oh, nonsense, Major. Donald. I read a full account in a magazine. You were, you are a hero.'

'It's not like that, Mary.'

When he sees my questioning look, he adds, 'You don't want to believe all the hype. It all happens so quickly you don't even think. We were all in it. The noise and dust and heat and sand. We helped each other. I happened to be coming home, end of my tour, and they wanted some press. This whole bloody circus starts to churn and spits you out as someone else. That's why we're going on holiday, get back to reality. Now if you really don't mind…'

In the end they didn't want my apple pie. She said she had balaclavas for dessert that wouldn't keep. I didn't like to ask what they were, foreign, no doubt. They were leaving in the morning so would have to use them up.

'Another time. You must come for supper and we'll share one of your apple pies then. Perhaps I could have the recipe.'

I am back in my house, numb. I pick up the local paper. Nothing about him. He's old news. There's to be an antiwar protest at the war memorial on Saturday. I am encouraged to bring a musical instrument to promote peace and a healthy snack to share. I could take my apple pie, my white sugar, white flour, traditional apple pie and hurl it in their aloe-vera scrubbed faces.

Do you know, I think I'll go.

Madonnas

Excuse me, can I have a word? I want, actually I need to speak to you. Have you a minute or two? It's warm in here. They keep these shopping centres overheated, don't they?

What a lovely baby! He's not going to fret, is he? Good.

Lovely. Oh, *she*. You can't tell, can you? Not with the rainbow suit. What's her name? Aurora? How unusual... and what's yours? Samantha...but you like Sam. Lovely names. I'm Jessica, by the way.

I may be speaking out of turn... The thing is, I was shopping here earlier when you were handing out leaflets. I was hot so I took a break on one of the benches. I watched you. You were nervous, weren't you? Bucking up the nerve to approach people. I could see it in your face; you sort of froze just before you spoke. The baby made it easier. Even when they're sleeping, people just love to look at babies. It's like looking into the future. I saw them come up to you. That old man, the one who raged at you, did that upset you? Yes, I thought it did.

It used to upset me too.

Don't look so surprised.

That's what I wanted to speak to you about.

When I came by you looked at me, but you didn't hand me a leaflet.

No, don't be embarrassed. You don't need to apologise, either.

I'm not angry. I just wanted to know...was it my clothes or my face?

Do I look too old?

Were you afraid I would turn away?

81

I felt like that at the Faslane demos. I'm sure I did. With some people, you get a feeling, don't you? That they don't want to get involved, and they're angry with you for making them show it.

Is that what you felt coming from me?

You were just weary. Are you not getting enough sleep? Does she wake through the night still?

Not tired then. Weary. Weary of people's indifference.

Yes, I used to feel that. I just gave them a leaflet anyway to show my strength.

I was weak inside, like a baby.

Looking at the crowd, listening to the shouting. Feeling excited and afraid. Needing a pee every five minutes, not knowing if there were toilets.

Hundreds of policemen.

The military police...you couldn't see their eyes under their helmets.

American accents. They whispered obscenities at us. Horrible.

One time, there was an old man there (like the one that shouted at you), ex-army wearing medals, shouting at me, pointing at my baby in the pushchair. *Don't you care if he's killed by the bloody Russians?* He was so angry. I thought he might have a stroke. I tried to ignore him but he kept staring at my baby, and coming at me. *Why don't you take him out of the cold? What kind of mother are you? We fought a war for the likes of you, you scruffy bitch.*

Scruffy bitch! If I had a pound for each time I've been called that...

Oh, I know you wouldn't think it now looking at me but it was so exciting to dress like that. Bright colours, badges, it felt like the inside of your mind was on your outside. I dressed my son in red tights and an *angel top*, black gingham, like a smock. My mother nearly fainted. She knitted him piles of pastel cardigans but we had Babygro suits by then, yellow not lemon, royal not sky blue. At the creche on the mat they looked like a handful of jelly beans, even the babies glowed with life. We thought we could move mountains. I'm so glad I lived through that time.

I still feel the same inside.

Full of hope…in spite of everything.

Have you been on a big march?

Glasgow…two weeks ago?

Brilliant.

With Aurora?

Of course.

Yes, I took mine to Faslane and Greenham, lots of CND and Vietnam marches through the sixties and seventies. Everyone took their kids (a lot only had mothers). It felt like the world was growing. To be with hundreds of other people who cared for things outside themselves. Funny thing is, a lot of my generation want to forget they ever did that kind of thing, except for theme nights at the club. Then out come their pink and orange glad-rags. Odd how so many of them kept them. It's all aerobic classes and holidays now. Or pensions.

They don't like admitting that they ever cared.

I'm an embarrassment to them these days.

Your friends are like that too?

But you're standing here handing out leaflets to people, feeling nervous, no confidence.

And they screw them up, stuff them in their pockets, drop them on the ground...

Yes, I know, you've got to do something.

I've sent seventy-five e-mails to Westminster in the last two weeks, and a packet of cooked rice to feed the Iraqis.

Bugger all use probably. Pointless gesture. I can hear my dad saying it.

Your dad does too?

There's some days I don't know how far I am from taking a brick and throwing it through MacDonald's window, or the bank or the council offices.

Don't laugh...I would if I thought it would make a difference.

My husband says it's the mothering that does it. He says he'd rather take on a tiger than an angry mother.

So that's what I wanted to say to you.

When I think about it, I only wanted the world to be safe for my boys.

In old paintings the babies don't look any different from now. The mothers are the same apart from their clothes, and those haloes.

But it's in their faces...

Every mother has that Madonna somewhere in her soul and it makes us brave, or reckless, as my dad would have it.

Don't lose it, Sam.

Brave Boys

I must not watch the News, Julie told herself. The clock straightened to attention at six o'clock, she clicked the remote and the screen flashed into life.

There was another one of course, only one this night, nineteen years old. She flinched. A blurred face in camouflage, beret askew, sand all round. A boy called Barry. Three brothers, a fiancée, school friends of a year back and the parents, stunned, facing the cameras, not able to speak. A spokesman for the family said they were devastated. She took up her pencil and put a cross through the last four strokes on her list, making thirty-five this month. Someone ought to do something, she thought, something like we did at Faslane all those years ago.

She had been so frightened, by her father as much as the chance of being arrested. All because she said she was going to take Bobby.

'You go if you have to, but don't take the baby! What if you get arrested? Whatever are you thinking of, you silly girl?' His face was red. He didn't usually shout.

'I want him to have a future. I want them to see what harm they could do.'

Her father turned away. 'I fought a war for the likes of you. People died. Just so you could be free to say what you liked. What a bloody waste of time!'

This was her Daddy – Daddy who smelt of aftershave and pipe tobacco, whose navy uniform was scratchy against her cheek. Daddy who had embodied all that was safe and hopeful.

'You said I should say what I believe in.' She spoke to his shuddering back.

When he turned around he was fighting tears. Puffed up with resolve, she still wanted to run into his arms and be his darling Julie again. She was on the tipping point of doing it when he closed the conversation, bitter and cold.

'I didn't expect you to believe in rubbish.'

Where are they now, she wondered, all those young women growing old like me? Not likely to want to sit down in the road linking arms, singing, smiling into the faces of military men trying to disentangle them, not resisting but falling limp so they were dead weight. The military men had not been taught how to deal with the passive, except by whispering obscenities which they hadn't been taught either but which seemed to come easily. Julie had been surprised by the hatred in their eyes, or perhaps it was fear.

Once, a younger soldier with a child's complexion had tugged at her arm.

On impulse, she asked him, 'Don't you have a mother, sisters like me?'

He had recoiled from her as if from a hornet sting, dropping her arm. 'My mother, my sister, know how to behave, you fucking hippy cow!' The swearing sounded awkward, tacked on, but he was shaking with anger.

An older soldier beside him grabbed back her arm and spoke to the young one. 'Know what to do with these bitches? Fuck them, fucking fuck them. That'll shut them up.' He squeezed her arm hard.

She flinched. 'He'd do that to your mother and sister too,' Julie spat out, pulling away from his grip.

He dropped her arm, turned to the pushchair. 'This yours? Taking care of it, are you? Little bastard.'

He wrenched the pushchair towards him. Bobby was asleep but stirred at the sudden movement. Julie gasped and threw herself between him and the pushchair, howling. Two women on either side, dolphin like, sprang close. He was two feet taller than any of them but he stepped back.

'Fucking animals!'

Julie often looked back to that moment when peace had been the last thing on her mind. She might have tried to kill him if he hadn't backed off.

They used to taunt conscientious objectors with questions like that. What if they raped your mother, your sister, your daughter – would you fight then?

How can you know? she had wondered, but from that day, she had left Bobby at home.

Her mother had surprised her. Her father had been so furious, refusing to speak to Julie any more. She had crept around the house being anywhere that he wasn't – having breakfast early, lunch in her room and a cooling dinner in the kitchen after he had gone through to the sitting room to watch television. Her mother hovered between them, slipping into the kitchen to whisper to her and Bobby as she ate, but not for long. She heard them arguing about her, her mother appearing with reddened eyes.

The morning of a particular demo, as she was trying to leave the house quietly, her mother had come downstairs in her dressing gown and pressed a five pound note into her hand and whispered, 'Good luck, darling. You tell them.'

Julie wondered how far away her mother had been to grabbing her coat and going with them.

So, no current contact list. Not strictly true, she had a list of friends who played bridge, friends who were in the Book Club, friends who were in the Dance Fitness group and friends who were just friends. Julie couldn't think of a single one who had shared more than a passing word about the dead boys with her. 'Brave boys' was what they murmured. If she tried to continue the conversation they changed the subject. It was too emotional. In spite of being children of the Sixties, her friends didn't always 'let it all hang out' to one another but preferred talking about their good health, their slim figures, their active retirements, their tinted hair, their stretched faces. Julie thought it was possible that they didn't care any more than they had in the past when they had laughed at her, or despised her for being so serious.

One of them had laughed out loud and said, 'Oh, go and join something, Julie – go online and sign petitions or something – but shut up about the war. There's nothing we can do about it.'

Once she managed a conversation, with Bill, her regular dance partner, who had been in the army. They'd been at the pub after the dance session and the five o'clock news had come on the overhead television. Another nineteen-year old shot dead. They looked at the huge screen, at its sweep across a sandy landscape, then a photo of the dead soldier, Peter.

'Oh dear, not another one.' She had been close to tears.

Bill turned white. 'Oh dear Lord, that's a lad from the town. I know him. Used to work at the butchers. Nice lad. Sold me sausages.'

'How awful.' Julie pressed his hand.

'Bloody waste,' Bill said. 'They've hardly started. They should send old men to war.'

'I heard they don't have the proper equipment,' she said.

'I heard some of them buy their own to get decent stuff,' he added.

'No! Surely not.' Julie couldn't believe that.

'Into the desert without proper boots. The bloody government too bloody busy bailing out the banks!' he said before tipping the last of his beer down his throat.

In spite of Bill's non-sequitur, that was when Julie decided to do something.

I have to be realistic, she thought. I'm not brave enough to pour petrol on myself and burn outside the House of Commons and these days you can't get near the House in case you're a terrorist, but I might be able to do this. Bobby is expecting to inherit and there'll still be the house and it's not as if he's badly off.

The next night made her mind up. There had been three more on the news. Eddie, Jonathan and Robert. Twenty-one, twenty-nine and twenty-four years old. Eddie had ginger hair and supported Liverpool, Jonathan and Robert were both fathers of young children. Vehicle ran over a mine. Next of kin have been informed.

Is it worse, Julie wondered, to know that two other families are broken?

One step at a time, she thought, easy things first. She took a good long look at her bank balances. At £100 a day her savings would last for one hundred days. She would use the ATM so she wouldn't have to speak to anyone at the bank, not at first anyway. Who to pay it to concerned her. She was fairly sure that that the Army would have no bank account for donations and she couldn't choose a single soldier to support.

She didn't know any army families. What if she asked the local press to start a fund? There was a twice-weekly paper, *The Ayrshire Press*, that covered news across the region and had previously run campaigns on local issues. She phoned the editor.

They agreed there would be no coverage until she'd made the first week's payments. Julie laughed when he said there was always a chance she might be a nutter with no money but she saw his point. There must be so many people, sincere people, who would like to do something but never got round to it. Newspapers don't report small failures, she thought. That Monday afternoon, she threaded her way through the shoppers, withdrew her first £100 and took it to the newspaper office. It took ten minutes between bank and office and afterwards she chuckled at babies in prams and smiled at the young men chatting by the shop next to the bank.

Come Friday, she felt quite excited as she set off for her fifth trip. On Monday she would work with the editor on a centre-spread. He thought it stood every chance of snowballing – a local fund for local soldiers would make it real – people are more inclined to give to a cause for something they can identify with. Peter's funeral was due to be held that week, bound to be a huge turnout, television even, he had mused

It was raining and the street was quieter than usual. People dashed between shops but the young men were there, huddled under the shelter of the bank's pediment, hoods up against the rain. She made her transaction, dropped the notes into her handbag and replaced her card in her purse.

She turned away from the bank and started towards the newspaper office.

She felt their presence like a warm hug, two beside, two behind, before they guided her sideways into an alley between the buildings. The two beside her lifted arms and fast walked her deeper into the alley towards a pile of huge catering bins. They pushed her against the wall. One of them was sniggering.

'Don't scream. Shhhh.'

'Give us the notes.'

Julie's knuckles were white. One of them saw that.

'Don't muck about. Give us the bag.'

'Take it, Ash.'

'Shuttup. No names.' In turning, his hood slipped off his head. Julie saw his face.

He didn't care. Julie was back at Faslane.

'Wait,' she said.

'Give us the fucking bag.'

'I will. If you let me speak.'

'Just take it. Cut it off her. Here.'

There was a glint of metal.

'It's leather. You won't cut it with that,' Julie said. 'Let me speak.'

'Fuck off, lady. It'll cut you.'

He moved forward. The one called Ash put an arm out.

Julie shivered. 'Let me speak.'

'Go on then – one minute,' Ash said.

'This money is for equipment for soldiers. Boys like you.'

'Fucking Boys!'

'Go on,' Ash said.

'They're dying every day.'

'More fucking fools them.'

'Army twats.'

'Go on,' Ash said.

'They don't have the right equipment.'

'Is that it?' Ash asked.

Julie slumped against the wall. They stood around her, smelling of sweat and aftershave with a bass note of darker intent emanating from them. The sniggering one twitched, looking over his shoulders back down the alley. Ash stared at her hard, looking like her angry father and the young American MP at Faslane at the same time. There was disgust in his eyes.

'You old hippy,' Ash sneered, each word larded with hatred.

She dropped her bag. Ash tipped it up, pocketed the cash and threw it back at her feet. He gestured to the others to follow, walked halfway back down the alley before whispering something to the one who had sniggered, the one with the knife. He turned back.

Julie woke to the flicker of a television screen above her. Two dead soldiers, uncounted number of casualties in an accidental hit on a twenty-first birthday party, a government spokesman says it's all going very well, all things considered. She dozed in and out of several more news bulletins before she saw Bobby sitting quietly beside her.

'Hello,' she whispered.

'Mum.'

He looked so strained. How long has it been?

'Shall I fetch a nurse?' said Bobby.

'No. Just stay. What day is it?'

'Saturday. It's been a week.'

'Was I bad?'

'Yes.'

'Can't feel anything. Have they cut anything off?'

'No. You're sedated. Knife wounds are painful. Oh Mum...' Bobby was crying, bent over her bed but she couldn't reach him.

'Don't Bobby, don't. I'm all right.'

His sobbing softened. He took a deep breath and straightened. 'We want you to come and live with us.'

'Don't be daft. That would be awful.'

'You're not that bad.'

'No, you. You'd drive me nuts.'

'Mum, you can't go on like this.'

'Like what?'

'Doing mad things. Taking risks. These causes. You're getting old.'

Julie sighed. 'You never did care for what went on in the world, Bobby.'

'Don't start that. I just don't share your views.'

'You're like your granddad.'

'Well, he wasn't so bad.'

Julie turned away. 'I'm tired now. Can you let me sleep?'

Bobby got up and kissed her cheek. 'We'll talk some more. Goodnight.'

No matter how hard Bobby nagged and the women police officers persuaded, Julie wouldn't talk to any of them. She had a problem with uniform, Bobby told them, well aware how lame it sounded. She'd been trying to help young soldiers, kids in uniform, one of them observed. It was a problem with authority, he corrected himself. The young policewoman raised her eyebrows and asked if Julie wasn't a bit, well, old to have that kind of attitude. Bobby looked apologetic. She'd always been that way, bit of a serial protester. They told Bobby they knew the lads that had mugged Julie, recognised them from their habit of hanging about in the shopping precinct, but without witnesses and with paper money...

Julie dreamed about Ash. Sometimes he was in the army, a corporal, in charge of a bunch of scared nineteen year olds, a natural leader commanding with his voice unless something more physical was needed. In her dreams Ash led his patrol towards some dreadful danger, broken buildings perfect for snipers, ground soft enough for mines. They were armed and armoured but heads are soft and limbs get blown off from beneath. Julie woke up just before the explosion wondering if she feared it would happen or wished it would happen.

At other times Ash was lurking in dark places with his mates, intent on malice, watching her, pointing at her, directing them towards her. She minded his cool leadership far more than she minded the sniggering one's careless violence. From these dreams she woke sweating. Ash, the soldier, and Ash, the lout, became hard to separate in her mind. Sometimes he was among the dusty soldiers on the television back from some tense patrol among silent, resentful inhabitants. What he had done to her would be hardly worthy of notice there.

There were a series of furious arguments with Bobby. He was cruel in his frustration, told her she'd never grown out of her reckless student behaviour, was irresponsible, selfish and thoughtless and an embarrassment to them. Her convalescence with his family was fraught. The final straw came when he overheard her interpreting the television news to her fourteen-year old granddaughter. A month after the mugging, Julie moved back, still tender where she'd been stabbed and tearful when she thought about it, but ecstatic to be home.

That night she ordered three reinforced motorbike security chains at £100 each from the internet that were described as being highly resistant to hacksaws and bolt-cutters. She would wear a skirt for reasons of modesty – no protective ring of women this time to shield her peeing into a plastic jug – and eat a packet of prunes to clear herself out before she went to the town hall with its beautiful iron railings. Once the chains had arrived she phoned the editor and told him what she planned. He was delighted and promised to send a photographer.

Julie sat on the floor with a fistful of marker pens and a huge placard. She'd pencilled in *Stop the War* but it looked a bit lame. It wasn't quite what she wanted to say. Through the evening she tried lots of other wordings, but they all sounded like worn out cries from the past.

She thought about Faslane and about her baby, Bobby and the rough raw anger of the military police. She thought about Ash and his anger, about the sniggering one and his callow obedience.

Finally she wrote and was satisfied. When she left the house the next morning with her basket of chains, pee jug, sandwiches and thermos she carried a placard that said,

Let our baby boys be gentle.

Let them work that out, she thought.

Sorting Office

Without uniform there was no way to keep them together, or separate. Clothes blow off much easier than limbs and there were more than enough feet, legs, hands and arms lying in the sand to make identification, to make reunion, problematic. Easier if you had the head. She didn't always know if she had gathered all of one body or not. She imagined that they would mind an enemy foot in their coffin. She felt uneasy doing it by skin tone but there was no DNA analysis within a thousand miles, so she did what she could by intense visual scrutiny. If she was uncertain she made an aesthetic judgement, whether a hand or a foot was shapely enough, had well-shaped nails, had pale soles or palms. The pale freckled ones were easy. Tattoos with Kimberly or Shaz definitive, the Asian Brits were the hardest. Sometimes she went by how well fed the flesh was – the enemy were short of food – but she knew about metabolism, it was hardly fail-safe.

A recent one was troubling her more than most. A small young male Asian body assembled after a bombed building collapse. Both arms gone at first but then two squaddies brought in separate offers – a left and a right found a hundred metres apart in the rubble. Matching sizes, amputation points and skin tone but on the left wrist a tattoo, 'Marty', on the right wrist a woven band with intricate Arabic letters. She couldn't sign him off. All that day she tried to picture Marty, a boy's name, surely not an Asian name. She looked at the woven band. His mosque? His betrothed? In the evening by lamplight she copied the lettering and sent it by motorbike to HQ.

It came back the next day.

'Made in Birmingham'

She zipped the body bag shut, wrote Intact on the label and called for the orderly.

How to Be A War Widow

I don't know how to do this. I am playing a part I have seen on television. I am wearing black, carrying flowers. My sister carries our toddler son. Jack's brother is beside me, his mother beside him. I steal a look at her to copy her expression but her face is blank. That may be the tranquillisers. Our eyes cannot meet for fear of tears. I heard someone whisper look at that sweet little boy and say how dignified we all are. I do not feel dignified, just silent in case someone realises that I am not sure what I am feeling. I look around rows of faces, some men who were once soldiers and widows of such men but mostly strangers drawn here by news of a funeral. Two 'Loved Ones'. There is another small group, supporting a young woman in black. Her hat shrouds her face. The spectators hold flags. We are waiting for the signal to walk. I am not thinking that Jack was brave and noble, gave his life for his country trying to secure democracy for the Iraqi people. I am thinking of Jack my lover whose powerful body is in pieces in a box behind me and he will never take me to bed again. The other family wait beside their box. We do not speak.

How selfish I am. I don't care that Jacklet – we call him that to distinguish father from son – will not know his father. Jack was away for all but six weeks of his infancy. He was all promise – of football games, learning to ride a bike, swimming... he held the baby as if it were an unexploded bomb – oh heavens, gallows humour at this moment not required – and said with a sorry smile, 'I'll be fine once he's walking.'

Right now, thinking of Jack, I feel that pang in my body that the sight of his naked body always caused – even if we'd rowed, even if he was drunk – the breadth of his back, the length of his thighs, his belly hairs. I must stop this. If all these people knew what I was thinking, standing here waiting to walk Jack to his grave, they'd think I was a complete tart, not worthy of a hero, not good enough to be the mother of his son. I can't help it. I won't think of the other stuff.

I didn't see his body.

'Best not,' the sergeant said. 'Think of him how he was.'

That's because he's not all there. I can't imagine what happens to a human being when a device goes off under his foot. Is a device less dramatic than a bomb or a booby trap? What about an improvised explosive device, which sounds as if it were something admirable, something clever?

It turned out to be a metal drainpipe, packed with explosive and a detonator, set off by a pressure mat – a bit more lethal than something the delinquents on the estate might cook up to plague the corner shop Asians with. Don't suppose they ever quite got round to pressure mats but there you are, Jack just walked onto it.

'You can be proud of him,' the sergeant added.

For what exactly?

Perhaps if I assemble all the bits of feeling I'll end up with something comprehensible, something worthy of him, something to lay at his grave other than these flowers. He hated flowers. They gave him hay fever so I had to carry silk flowers at the wedding and all the church and reception

100

flowers had to be the same. Cost us a fortune. So what have I got?

Anger.

With the army for sending him over there, for not having detectors. Anger with him for not looking where he was going, for not being second in line to enter the village. Anger with the insurgents for...for what...resisting people they saw as invaders? That's how his brother saw it. I don't know enough to know if I feel that.

Loss.

I've lost my lover, my husband, Jacklet's father. Income, our army home (I don't want to stay there now – all those other sympathetic wives). I might go home to Mum and Dad, until I think it all out. She'll look after Jacklet any time I want to go out, but where would I go? Can't go clubbing with the girls. We've separated into the ones who've got married and the ones who are still free. Free – that's a laugh – they all want to be married but not to a dead soldier.

There's a girl about my age on the edge of the pavement crying. She's not official. She'd be over here with us if she was. Not wearing black either but she's crying hard, shoulders going up and down with her sobs. The people around are not comforting her, maybe they're strangers, but she's crying on and the tears flow down her cheeks and make a damp patch on her pink top.

I wonder who she is. A girlfriend not in deep enough to be engaged? Can't be a close relative. Cousin maybe? Not sure if that's a wife with the other family, just a sagging mother and three who might be brothers. What if she was Jack's bit on the side? I know from the other Army wives that it's best not to ask about how they cope with sex when they're away – but he shouldn't have needed anyone else here. I'm suddenly angry with the girl on the pavement. She looks over at me, stops crying and manages a watery smile. I glare at her, the bitch. Who does she think she's smiling at? Shall I stride across and slap her – give her something to cry about? What does it matter now?

We're off. The army people have arranged themselves behind and between the two hearses. An officer approaches our small party and indicates where we should walk. We shuffle into place – me in front, my sister and Jacklet beside Jack's mother behind, his brother bringing up the rear. The soldiers wear their caps low on their brows, you can't see their eyes. Is it in case they should laugh? Jack told me they laugh all the time out there, tell each other filthy jokes, but they don't mean it badly. It's not as if they can talk about what's really happening to them. We move into the street and there are hundreds of faces turned towards the procession.

Their faces express infinite sorrow. They throw flowers under the wheels of the hearses and our feet. I hear Jacklet chuckle behind me as he sees the promise of a game amongst all this strangeness. He tries to catch the falling flowers, struggling in my sister's arms, so I turn and take him and hold him close to my body. His struggles cease, his face puckers and he starts to cry.

'Shhh, Jackie – shhh. We'll find an ice-cream man later,' I whisper.

His eyes inspect mine for sincerity. I don't blink.

I see the television commentator keeping pace with me. He whispers into his microphone. He can't hear me but I know he is telling the country that I am comforting my infant son after the loss of his brave father. Maybe I am. Maybe the prospect of an ice cream means more to Jacklet than the memory of Jack, a near stranger who was a rival for his mum's attention. Maybe he won't miss him at all. Certainly the tears have dried and he walks holding my hand and the crowd's hearts will be in their mouths at such a sweet spectacle.

Now I can see the town clock. Two o'clock. The last time I saw the clock at that hour was in the early morning staggering home after a twenty-first party, both of us fairly pissed, me carrying my shoes, Jack trying to carry me and the pair of us hopeless with laughter. Laughter and sudden lust, so he pushed me into a deep doorway and, in the moonlight in the middle of town against someone's doorway, made rough and wonderful love. Three years ago. Probably the night that Jacklet was conceived though, to be truthful, it could have been any night that month, but that's how we liked to think of it.

Pain courses through me. My breath comes in short spasms as I close this circle. I look around for Jack, then remember he is the only one who is not here.

It's done. I stand a little way off from the crowd of soldiers and mourners, the council officials and the three ministers. My sister has taken Jacklet for the promised ice cream, a double one since he was patient and uncomplaining through the short service. There is a wooden bench and a birch tree beside me, its delicate leaves trembling in the breeze, throwing a scatter of shadows over the grass. They are mesmerising so I watch them.

'Could I have a word?'

A young woman. I don't know her but she looks familiar. She indicates the bench so I sit down and she follows.

'My name is Beth,' she says.

'Are you from the BBC? Or the papers?' It's all I can think to ask. She doesn't carry a tape recorder or a notebook. Perhaps she has a good memory.

'No. Mine was the other one.'

So she was the wife. She had a hat on before.

'It's awful, isn't it?' she says.

'Yes.' But I don't know whether she means today and all this or our dead husbands and all that.

'All of it.'

She must be telepathic. We sit in silence until the breeze turns chilly. After a while she glances at the crowd by the graves and turns to me.

'Shall we slip away? Will your little boy be all right?'

I can't think of any reason to stay. My sister will take care of Jacklet and not worry about me, at least until tonight. I'd rather share silence with Beth than talk nonsense to the crowd. So we walk down the path, two widows in black, back to the town where a road sweeping vehicle is sucking up flowers and the pavements are empty of people. The BBC van has gone.

'Do you want to talk about him?' she asks and though I knew I could, I said, 'Not now,' and she replies, 'Me neither.'

We walk on together past the pubs where the soldiers gather to laugh and net girlfriends, walking away from the laughing girls we were towards the women we must become.

Also Available from Pewter Rose Press

Amelia and the Virgin by Nicky Harlow
    Paperback ISBN 9780956005397
    ebook ISBN 9781908136046

Liverpool,1982. A darkly comic tale of a cult surrounding a visionary adolescent in Liverpool, who believes she is pregnant with the new Messiah. Fast-paced and grimly baroque, this is a wickedly funny tale of religious hysteria, human duplicity and corrupted innocence.

...a master class in writing...compelling. Bookbag

...Nicky Harlow's deftly-plotted novel is peopled by a cast of eccentric characters...The story's dominant mood is comic, but darker shadows are visible beneath the lightness of the writing. Lynda Prescott

...a very accomplished novel. Paul Magrs

Standing Water by Terri Armstrong
    Paperback ISBN 9781908136008
    ebook ISBN 9781908136121

Winner of the 2010 Yeovil Literary Prize (pre-publication).
When Dom returns to the Western Australian Wheatbelt for his mother's funeral after eight years away, he is shocked to find a region on the verge of collapse, devastated by drought and salinity.

A completely engaging and particularly vivid story, about friends and family, love and death...The setting is as vivid as the principal characters...exceptional. Henry Sutton

A Penny Spitfire by Brindley Hallam Dennis

Paperback ISBN 9780956005373

ebook ISBN 9781908136107

October 1947. Derek Fitton listens to Charles Bury's dreams of a fairer, socialist world. Clive Dandridge entangles a troop of misfit children. Tom and Violet Ferryman run The Odd Dog pub, where Burma Sammy drinks away his demob money, while Maria clacks across level crossings in her high heels.

...a rare glimpse into a time often forgotten in our accounts of victory. Janni Howker

...a very original novel, in subject matter and form. Frances Thimann

...Dennis's prose pulses with sensory detail...Writing of this quality is as hard to find as a penny spitfire on a bombsite. Nicky Harlow

The Onion Stone by Mandy Pannett

Paperback ISBN 9781908136015

ebook ISBN 9781908136138

Ardie Davendish and T.Townsend Ellis, have spent a lifetime striving to outdo each other with a literary 'scoop' about Shakespeare. Interwoven with their rivalry is an Elizabethan love story surrounding Gilbert Shakespeare and Anne Cecil. Secrets about the identity of Shakespeare are gradually revealed, leading to the final revelation.

...long-burning rivalry...passion and jealousy,...in masterful delivery. Douglas Pugh

...an extraordinary story....a rich and wide-ranging read. Roselle Angwin

The Secret's in the Folding by Fiona Thackeray

Paperback ISBN 9780956005366

ebook ISBN 9781908136206

Welcome to the world of Brazil – a country of colours and contrasts. The characters in these stories all show spirit, whether they are newly freed slaves, a beauty on a beach or dancers in Carnaval. Each story is a gem, but together they build up a mosaic image of Brazil and its characters.

...perfectly pitched evocation of Brazilian parasols and confit heaven in 'The Secret's in the Folding.' Suhayi Saadi

...'Mango'...tugs at your heartstrings however immune you think you are. Michael Faber

...'The Celestine Recipe'...an affecting, gentle humour, and is a genuinely mouth-watering read. Janice Galloway

November Wedding by Frances Thimann

Paperback ISBN 9781908136299

ebook ISBN 9781908136305

By the author of ***Cello and Other Stories***

'I had no plans to marry, my career lay comfortable and predictable before me; but seeds beneath the dry sands can be awakened with rain after thirty years, and so it was with me. And in spite of all that happened, and even now, so many years later, the feelings in my heart have not changed or diminished.'

Simply stunning. Megan Taylor

...very pleased to see a new collection by her. Ross Bradshaw

Brushstrokes by Heather Shaw

    Paperback ISBN 9781908136275

    ebook ISBN 9781908136282

The stories in Heather Shaw's first collection explore how we see ourselves and how others see us. Ranging from an 18th Century cleric juggling with his conscience, through a surreal cleaning experience and a collection of everyday objects, to an artist revealing his true feelings in his paintings, the stories show the gaps between what is said and what is felt.

…Predictive Text…*witty and beautifully written…immaculately presented – vivid characters.* Maggie Smith

…Total Immersion…*well written. The details are fascinating… And Gran is a wonderful character.* Wendy Cope, Guest Editor, Mslexia

Lightning Source UK Ltd.
Milton Keynes UK
UKOW031246060213

205912UK00006B/92/P